# Never Say Never

Anthony M.

T0329440

an imprint of

PUBLISHERS

expanding minds

x

www.longhornpublishers.com

1

Published by **Sasa Sema** Publications
*An imprint of Longhorn Publishers*

Longhorn Kenya Ltd.,
Funzi Road, Industrial Area,
P.O. Box 18033-00500,
Nairobi, Kenya.

Longhorn Uganda Ltd.,
Plot 731 Mawanda Road, Kamwokya
P.O. Box 24745,
Kampala, Uganda.

Longhorn Publishers (T) Ltd.,
Kinondoni Plot No. 4
Block 37B, Kawawa Road
Dar es Salaam, Tanzania.

© Anthony Mugo

All rights reserved. No part of this publication may be reproduced, stored
in a retrieval system or transmitted in any form or by any means, electronic,
mechanical, photocopying, recording or otherwise without the prior written
permission of the copyright owner.

First published 2012

**ISBN  978  9966 36 237 1**

Cover illustration by Tuf Mulokwa

Printed by Printwell Ltd., off Enterprise Road, Industrial Area,
P.O. Box 5216 - 00506, Nairobi, Kenya.

# Foreword

The National Book Development Council of Kenya (NBDCK) is a Kenyan non-governmental organisation made up of stakeholders from the book and education sectors. It is mandated to promote the love of reading, the importance of books and quality education.

In November 2010, the NBDCK partnered with the Canadian Organisation for Development through Education (CODE) to introduce in Kenya the Burt Award for African Literature, which involves identification, development and distribution of quality storybooks targeting the youth.

The purpose of the Burt Award books such as *Never Say Never* is to avail to the reader quality, engaging and enjoyable books whose content is portrayed in an environment the reader can easily identify with, thereby arousing his/her interest to read and to continue reading. This sharpens the reader's English language and comprehension skills leading to a better understanding of the other subjects.

The NBDCK would like to thank Bill Burt for sponsoring and allowing the Burt Award for African Literature to be introduced in Kenya. Special thanks also go to the panel of judges for their professional input into this project. Finally, this foreword would be incomplete without recognising the important role played by all the NBDCK stakeholders whose continued support and involvement in the running of NBDCK has ensured the success of the first Burt Award in Kenya.

**Ruth K. Odondi**

*Chief Executive Officer*
*National Book Development Council of Kenya*

# Acknowledgement

The Burt Award for African Literature recognises excellence in young adult fiction from African countries. It supports the writing and publication of high quality, culturally relevant books and ensures their distribution to schools and libraries to help develop young people's literacy skills and foster their love of reading. The Burt Award is generously sponsored by a Canadian philanthropist, Bill Burt, and is part of the ongoing literacy programmes of the National Book Development Council of Kenya, and CODE, a Canadian NGO which has supported development through education for over fifty years.

# CHAPTER 1

"Happy new year!" the teacher said.

"Happy new year!" the class thundered back.

"You are now in standard four. Congratulations!" our new class teacher said, overriding the murmur in the class. The end of the holidays was never welcomed with a smile. It meant waking up early, less time to play, and following a restraining schedule. Nevertheless, it was 1986, a brand new year, and for the lucky ones, it meant graduating to the next class. I was now in upper primary!

Memories of days gone by flooded my mind. I recalled my first day in school and smiled. That day always brought a smile to my lips. The interview entailed passing the left hand over the head to touch the right ear. Well, I am yet to discover the correlation between the length of a hand, the head and education. Anyway, that was the rule of thumb back in those days. Doomed were the children with big heads and short arms. I was six years old. Either my head was too big or my arm too short because I happened to be one of the doomed ones. My mother was determined to get me enrolled, so she stretched my arm to the hilt and made me hold it in place. That was painful, of course, and I sobbed silently. By the time the interviewer got to me, I had let go. She simply looked at me and told me to go home. My mother hit the roof. The teacher told her that arguing would not change anything.

"His arm is short. We cannot argue about that," the teacher said.

I ran all the way home because my mother thrashed me with a cane whenever she caught up with me. She did not utter a word on the way home. I could hardly see why she was so mad. To my young mind, it was much ado about nothing. I could not figure out why school was so important. If anything, I had just earned myself extra time to play with other children.

Unfortunately for me, very few interviewees made it through that year and, consequently, rules were relaxed. According to the interviewer, I had almost passed and, to my disappointment, I was enrolled two days later.

"We will begin with introductions," the teacher was saying. "Let us start from this end."

"Peter Njoroge Kamau," the boy seated near the door said.

"Anastasia Njeri Munene," his desk mate thundered.

I found myself among forty other pupils in nursery school. The classroom was mud-walled and we dutifully sprinkled water on the floor to contain the dust.

Somebody had carefully studied our environment and recommended a soil-brown uniform.

Adapting to school life was not easy. It was like domesticating a wild animal. It was a completely new experience: waking up at six and braving the morning cold, learning the alphabet and numbers, drawing my mother on the ground and singing *Baa, Baa, Black Sheep* and *London's Burning*. However, with time, I created new friendships and found the things we learnt in class very interesting.

When you looked at the school compound on an off day, it looked like a stalled project. There was no gate at the entrance, the classrooms had neither doors nor windows and the newly built standard eight classes were yet to be roofed. The nursery section was still mud-walled. To the left of the compound were pit latrines, some perilously sunk into the ground and many without doors. A repulsive urea stench hung stubbornly about them. To the right was the playground, with tall cypress trees lining its perimeter. It had a poor topography and only the two goal posts made of timber suggested some games were played there.

A visit on a morning when the school was on, however, would have revealed a spectacle to behold. One would have seen the children proudly streaming from far and near, some of them panting from running in their zest to keep time. Evidently, many parents were as eager as my mother to educate their children, judging by the high population; each class had two streams.

"Your name?" the teacher's voice pulled me out of my reverie. It was my turn to introduce myself. I got to my feet, an act that attracted subdued giggles. I hesitated as my eyes surveyed the class involuntarily, resting on Anastasia. She was the most beautiful girl in our class and I was attracted to her. Indeed, as far as I could surmise, every boy was attracted to her and all girls were envious of her beauty.

"Do you have a name?"

"Muthini Njoki," I quipped bravely.

The class had been pregnant with laughter and immediately I mentioned my name, it exploded. It exploded because Njoki was my mother's name. It was an invitation to ridicule for a boy to bear a female name. Having no husband and with a son who was not baptized, my mother had enrolled me using her name. I had no reason to hate my classmates; I was only embarrassed. They had fathers and were baptized, and I didn't expect them to understand what it meant to lack any of these. To them, it was just a chance for a good laugh. Personally, I could not understand why I had no father or was not baptized.

They also laughed at my uniform. My shorts were patched at the rear, my sweater at the elbows and my shirt at the shoulders and collar. My mother was an expert in needlework, doing all the patchwork at home.

My hesitation and the resulting laughter seemed to bother our new class teacher. He waited long enough for the laughter to ebb out then said, "Is there anything awkward or funny?" He turned to me. "That is a wonderful name! Back at home, they call me Wa Njambi. Njambi is my loving mother and I am very proud of her. The name reminds me that whereas some people don't have a mother, God has blessed me with one. You should be proud of yours, too." He turned to the class, "Here in school, call me Mr. Mate."

I was so impressed by my new class teacher I felt like crying. For the first time, I found myself counting my blessings. What if I didn't have a mother?

My classmates did not bother me as much as Mr. Maringa, the headmaster. In fact, I dreaded him. I was a disciplined pupil and my academic performance was excellent because I was always among the top four. But then I was always on his list of building funds defaulters and pupils in torn uniforms. The headmaster read out this list during the morning parade. I featured so regularly that I developed survival tactics. A few days after being sent packing, I would sneak back to school.

Four weeks after opening school, Mr. Mate was busy telling us about a hero called Koitalel arap Samoei when the headmaster stormed our class. He was burly with the temper of a wounded rhino. He was always in Kaunda suits and Travolta boots and always combed his short hair backwards. He did not apologise for the intrusion. He surveyed the sea of young faces looking at him with dreaded anticipation.

Suddenly, sweat started dripping from under my armpits. I had been suspended because of fees arrears a week before and now I was back. I had run into him that very morning when he asked my name. It was rumoured that he was poor in remembering faces and I lied straight to his face. They say the guilty are afraid. I shrank between my desk mates the best way I could but it wasn't good enough.

"You!" he echoed, pointing a thick index finger at me. "Come here!"

I stood, my legs trembling. I stumbled to the front, dozens of pairs of eyes riveted on me. I was trembling all over now, more from the realisation of how reckless my lie had been than from its aftermath. The headmaster had every right to be mad and I deserved to be punished.

"What is your name?" Someone giggled.

"Muthini Njoki."

"What did you tell me your name was?"

Frankly speaking, I could not recall. Even if I could, I was so terrified my voice had gone mute.

"Did you pay your building fund arrears?"

I shook my head. "Pack all your belongings and follow me."

I took my home-made bag and stuffed the few books and a fountain pen inside. I followed the headmaster to his office, seriously considering running off to solicit help from my mother. At the office, he flipped through a file, finally settling on one of the pages. He scanned it for a while and then he exploded, "My goodness! You were sitting in class comfortably and you still have last year's balance! You think this is a refugee camp, eh?"

He stared at me for a long moment, shaking his head in fury. I was in for a thorough beating. My heart was beating hard against my rib cage and I was busy rummaging through my mind for a convincing explanation. Apparently, there was none. I had earned whatever was in store for me. He scribbled on a piece of paper and threw it at me furiously.

"There is your balance. If you don't have it in full, don't bother to come back. Ever! Get out of my sight!"

I opened my mouth to speak but he brushed me off with his hands. I stepped out of the office and began my long, tortuous journey home.

# CHAPTER 2

I sat outside our house deep in thought. It was almost two years after being kicked out of school. Patrick Gachukia, one of my cousins, had just had his lunch and was setting off for school. He seemed so buoyant that I was jealous of him. He had a special reason to be. He had everything I wished I had: a father, friends to play with and above all, he was going to school.

It was clear I would never see the inside of a classroom again. My mother had failed to raise the fee balance of Kshs. 570. She was out of her depth and had resigned to our fate. No apparent help was forthcoming; everyone was too busy grappling with their problems to be concerned about us. Even God had more urgent and grave businesses to attend to, or so it seemed.

Who was to blame for my woes? Was it fate? Where was the man who was supposed to be my father?

My mother had no formal education because she had spent her childhood looking after her father's cattle. Not that he could not afford to educate her; far from it. There was just no need to waste resources on someone who would only get married and become a housewife. All that was needed was to teach her how to serve her husband, look after babies and execute household chores.

A girl had no right to inherit her parents' property. She was expected to grow up, get a worthy suitor, fetch a handsome dowry and, with luck, acquire land and wealth elsewhere by virtue of marriage. Whoever came up with this wisdom either committed a gross oversight or was outright selfish. Indeed, this was the height of male chauvinism. It would have made sense if every girl got married and never divorced. The marriage institution was increasingly losing its salt with many a woman choosing to die single and divorce cases escalating every passing day.

Following my mother's divorce, she had nowhere else to go but to her mother's home. We lived in a two-room mud-walled house. One room was my grandmother's kitchen while the other was our bedroom. My grandfather died when I was two years old. My uncles were inherently traditional, because tradition gave them an upper hand in matters of inheritance; thus my mother would not inherit anything. We were *persona non grata* in our current home and the best we could do was to show gratitude for the room we had been given to live in.

My mother was going through one of the most difficult times. She became depressed and blamed everyone for our woes. With time, her bitterness became colossal. She stopped talking to anyone at home. She had acquired a piece of land at the public cemetery where we grew maize and beans. When we were not working on the land, we looked for menial jobs such as picking coffee, digging and weeding. In the evening, my mother would go to the village market to sell bananas. The proceeds from our labour were too meagre to sustain us.

It had been a week of tragedies. The market where my mother sold bananas was situated on a road reserve in front of shops. That Monday, a vehicle had veered off the road. The traders had been able to take off in time but their wares had been run over. On Tuesday, we went to the garden at the cemetery and my mother almost collapsed. Someone had harvested all the maize we had planted.

My mother was in such a foul mood we stayed indoors the whole of Wednesday. On Thursday afternoon, a vehicle arrived abruptly at our home. I was dying to see the occupants, but looking at my mother, I stayed put. The sound of the engine died out, survived by heavy tramping of boots coming towards our house. Then there was a loud, hurried knock.

"Anybody home?"

My mother opened the door. There were two men at the door and a third one in the government Land Rover.

"We have come for him. We want him to get an education."

My mother grabbed me, shouting at the top of her voice. She swung the door in an attempt to close it but one of the men held it in place. The other one grabbed me and carried me bodily to the Land Rover. It was already in motion when the third man jumped on board. It took off perilously, leaving my mother screaming and dazed.

# CHAPTER 3

The driver picked up speed as we joined the main road. Like every typical boy, I always enjoyed a vehicle ride, but I did not enjoy this one. I sat sandwiched between the two men at the back seat, crying. They talked and laughed freely and one of them had the guts to smoke a cigarette. Their casualness was unnerving, considering what they had just done.

Our destination, I later learnt, was the District Children's Services Office. I was taken inside the building and made to sit on a chair. At the table was a man with a receding hairline and traces of grey hair. For reasons best known to him, he seemed pleased to see me.

"You are older than I thought," he observed with a smile. He stretched his hand to greet me but I ignored him. His smile broadened. "I don't blame you. One day you will understand."

He turned to the two gentlemen. "Well, take him across for the night."

I was escorted outside the building and into the evening sun. We walked outside the gate; then an alarm went off in my mind. We were heading for the police station! I yelled as the two men lifted me up and deposited me behind the reception desk inside the police station. At the desk sat an officer wearing his cap almost to his eyes.

"I have a guest for you," one of the men declared.

"No worry. We have plenty of bed space."

Police officers were moving in and out of the station calling one another 'Afande.' Some were in overcoats and they slung guns down their shoulders. One of the men who had brought me was left recording in a big book on the counter and the two walked out of the station. The officer at the reception lifted his eyes off the huge black book he was working on to study me carefully.

"Surrender all your money, one shoe and belt." I wondered if he had really seen me because I had none of these. Indeed, I never had them. Just then, another officer stormed in with a man I assumed they had arrested. The man was thrust forward. He fought to regain his balance but the officer's boot connected with his bottom and he fell flat on his face. A chill ran up my spine.

"I said one shoe and belt!" the officer at the table shouted, startling me. I had believed that my former headmaster, Mr. Maringa, was the fiercest person on the face of the earth. However, looking at the two officers, I could not help feeling how mistaken I had been. I was too terrified to speak. The officer just looked at me as though he was seeing me for the first time.

The other man surrendered his money, one shoe and one belt. We were both marshalled into a corridor with doors to the left. The officer unhooked a bunch of keys off his trousers, selected a key and opened one of the doors. He roughly threw us inside and quickly locked the door.

I found myself in a small, dimly lit room. Darkness had almost engulfed the earth and the weak daylight made its way into the room through some grilled ventilations high above. At the corner was a plastic bucket. My roommate walked to the bucket, undid his fly and proceeded to urinate into it.

"One of these days, I will kill that rascal," he muttered while struggling with his fly. "Then he will know why they call me Kabangi."

He walked to the far corner, removed the solitary shoe, hit the floor and coiled into a foetal position. He placed the shoe under his head and went to sleep. Ten minutes later, he was snoring like a pig. I sat there staring at him in bewilderment. How could one adapt so quickly to such a situation? How could he manage to sleep? Did he actually mean he would kill the policeman?

Back at home, the police station was the place to avoid at all costs. I remember one of my uncles who was fond of imbibing illicit brews. He would then arrive home and cause a commotion, beating up his wife and picking a quarrel with anyone who came his way. Then one day, he was arrested for being drunk and disorderly. He spent two days at the police station and upon his release, he became a changed man. He dreaded another visit to the station.

The young ones were fond of experimenting and we would throw stones at telephone lines on our way from school. The tale was that the whining sound the wires produced when hit went all the way to the police station. Thus, we would run all the way home to avoid being arrested.

Well, that was in the past. Now, I was sitting on the floor of a police cell. What had I done to warrant an arrest? Police cells house outlaws. Was I an outlaw? Someone somewhere must have been seriously mistaken to arrest me. I was the wrong person. It had to be.

A short while later, there was the sound of an approaching vehicle. The noise from its engine died out, leaving raised voices giving rapid-fire orders accompanied by the thumping of feet. The name 'Afande' was repeated several times and I wondered what it meant. A while later, I heard footfalls along the corridor, which stopped outside my door. The padlock to our cell rattled and the door flew open. A dozen or so men rushed inside the cell.

"You, come here," the policeman bellowed at me. "You will sleep here," he said, pointing at the corridor.

Falling asleep was a problem because of the cold. There was commotion in the middle of the night. Apparently, a new team was coming in, and the commotion meant a handover. The following day at nine, we were paraded in twos. We walked in a single file and I was shocked to discover that our destination was the Law Court. It made me more confused. We were then locked up in a small room that held gallons, electronics, furniture, three bicycles and many other items which Kabangi said was police evidence. This was a holding place for suspects when the court was in session, I thought. The first man was called, only to return twenty minutes later, crying.

"Oh God, one year!" he sobbed. Inmates that went after him received stiff sentences and huge fines, and word went round that the judge was in a foul mood. I was among suspects, the fact that I knew I was innocent notwithstanding. I found myself formulating my defence. This was not easy because I did not know what crime I had committed. By two, only Kabangi and I remained. Kabangi was called first and he returned ten minutes later smiling broadly. I interpreted his smile to mean the judge's foul mood had thawed. Now I was sure it was my turn. My heart beat faster and I started sweating profusely. I was about to face a judge! I was eagerly waiting to know what crime I had committed.

My turn to face the judge never came. Instead, an officer in plain clothes took me across town towards the bus station. We boarded a bus to Murang'a. "This is your new home," the policeman said as we went through a gate with a sign, 'Murang'a Juvenile Remand Home'. This new development further threw me off-balance. Had I been jailed already? How could they jail me after denying me a chance to face the judge and plead my case, if any?

As I came to learn later, the remand was a waiting facility for suspects pending court action. Usually, one would take fourteen days between court appearances. Rarely did one make more than three appearances.

Life here took a predictable course. In the morning, we took porridge. Police officers came at eight for those going to court. The rest of us went to work in the fields, which were infested with repulsive black jacks. We took our lunch at noon. In the afternoon, we would either play or sleep.

An escape from here was impossible. When we were outside the dormitory, we stayed in a wire mesh enclosure of about fifty square feet. There were always two members of staff on duty. To the north was a thicket that ran down to Mathioya River. The road was slightly visible over the thicket, at the bridge.

.

The dormitory was one big room. At one end, a stone barrier had been built to hide two raised stones and a bucket placed between them. This acted as the toilet. There were no beds. We slept in two opposite rows, on mats and covered ourselves with blankets. One blanket could cover as many as three boys.

Every place has a celebrity of some sort. Here, Karanchu was the one. He had been born in the streets of Nairobi and raised there. He knew the city like the back of his hand. At one time, he told me he had been admitted to Mama Ngina Children's Home. According to him, life there was too dull and he had escaped. He had been arrested in the city and confined in a remand home. He had managed to escape and, realising that the city was becoming too hot for him, he had decamped to Murang'a, where he had committed a crime and was promptly arrested. He was a confessed thief who could snatch such valuables as wrist watches, purses or necklaces in broad daylight and disappear into thin air. His experiences, frankness and flair made the rest of us envious. While others claimed innocence, he laid bare his criminal activities as though they were some trophies to be displayed. Karanchu was ever smiling to the world, while stress was slowly killing the rest of us. He walked with a carefree swagger. When he was not narrating his street exploits, he was talking about movies. He talked of such characters as Spiderman and Rambo.

After fourteen days, I was taken to court but did not face the judge. Instead, I was informed that they had secured a place for me in school. The news came as a relief. I was going back to school! Better still, the school was in the city. I pictured Kiambiriria Primary School with its windowless classrooms and felt sorry for those children who were still stuck there. I had always envied them, but now I pitied them. Very few people in my village had been to Nairobi. Most of them had imaginary and third-hand tales of skyscrapers and being lost in the big town. I was eleven and on the verge of being there in person.

That night was the longest night in my life. I had a strong resolve to stay awake because I imagined that if I slept, the big day would catch me unawares. I wanted to witness the big day unfold. However, slumber overcame me in the still of the night.

# CHAPTER 4

The big day dawned, but it brought disappointment with it. No one was in a hurry to begin the journey. For the first time, I was provided with breakfast at the police station: a slice of bread and a mug of very cold tea, with an overdose of tea leaves. I didn't enjoy it, mainly because my mind was elsewhere.

The sun was already high in the sky when we left. My escort for the journey was a tall, slender policeman in spectacles. He rarely talked throughout the journey. We boarded a Riakanau Bus. In the carrier, there was a mountain-load of unripe bananas.

The city was more spectacular than I had thought. The buildings were taller than I had imagined. Then there were things I had never imagined, like the traffic, both human and vehicular. Everyone was in a hurry. It was chaos. To my shock, there were soot-dark boys carrying equally dirty sacks. Some were sitting by tyre fires with bottles stuck in their mouths. The white of their eyes contrasted sharply with their oil-stained skin and resembled those of a cat in the dark. There were piles of filth on the alleys, on the road and in front of shops.

A cart full of unripe bananas zoomed past, missing me narrowly. I watched it in awe because, unlike back at home where carts were pulled by oxen and donkeys, here, a man was pulling it.

We had been walking for about ten minutes when I discovered we were going round in circles. I looked at my escort, who also appeared confused. He murmured something, then approached a newspaper vendor. He was given directions and within no time, we were boarding a matatu playing the loudest music I had ever heard. The conductor squeezed me between three tall men and I had difficulty breathing. At our destination, the police officer roughly pulled me and by the time I stepped out, my shirt had lost two buttons.

"Here we are," he declared. He took my hand and we crossed the road. The signboard pronounced: Getathuru Reception and Discharge Centre. After handing me over at the reception, the policeman left.

The first person I saw was Karanchu. He still had his carefree swagger.

The first hour gave me the shivers. It was like waking up and finding yourself in a lion's den. Two older boys were threatening to tear each other apart there and then. It was all about some amount of cash they had stolen and one had pocketed all the proceeds. Back at the Murang'a Remand Home, Karanchu had seemed a veteran, but here, he was seriously overshadowed.

The bell rang and we formed a queue. Food was served in bowls and placed on a table. I picked a bowl and surveyed its contents: beans and *ugali*. Immediately I placed the bowl on the table, a burly bearded man appeared and off-loaded my food into his bowl.

Just like at the remand, we slept early. Half a dozen of us slept on the floor. The rest had funny types of beds. They consisted of two metal bars which were folded to form equilateral triangles at both ends. Three pieces of timber were placed on top of the rods to form a bed.

By dawn, I was so hungry that I felt weak. I had missed meals the whole day. At seven, I had thick porridge for breakfast. I took it hastily, sticking near one of the staff members to avoid someone snatching my bowl once again. After breakfast, we were paraded in twos near the flag post. There was a heap of assorted farm implements: rakes, hoes and mattocks. A slender man in a track-suit and sports shoes was pacing in front meditatively. A boy, bigger than I, emerged from the dining hall. The slender man beckoned him with a crooked pointing finger.

"Time is what?" the man asked.

"Time is money!" It was a chorus.

"This is time for what?"

"*Fanya juu!*"

The boy approached him apprehensively. Once the boy was an arm's length away, the man's right foot caught him at the ankle and swept him off his feet with lightning speed. He landed on the ground like a sack of sugar.

"If you waste time, you get what?"

"Bullshit!"

I came to learn that the man in the track-suit was the farm master and the act he had just demonstrated was called 'bullshit.' Inmates had therefore nicknamed him Bullshit.

"Let's go," he bellowed.

Suddenly there was a stampede for the implements. Within no time, only the mattocks and hoes with a single spike were left.

"What are you waiting for? New hoes, eh?" It was the farm master. I quickly grabbed one of the mattocks. We walked in a file to the farm, where we embarked on weeding maize. The land sloped towards a valley, and gabions had been erected to arrest erosion. The farm manager was an athlete of a kind and he kept crisscrossing the big farm with ease. At about ten, there was a loud whistle. We were hurriedly grouped together and a roll call taken. Apparently, two inmates were missing. The farm master hurriedly left, accompanied by four huge boys and the rest of us were locked up in our dormitories.

The two escapees were arrested two hours later. They were stripped naked and table salt rubbed into their bottoms before being awarded the famous Six Strong Ones. They were called so because the strokes of the cane were executed by six of the strongest boys. They were tough because the following day, the two inmates were still struggling to walk.

Now I was sure all was not well. I discovered that all the talk about getting me back to school was but a pack of lies. I should have known. Why, it was a bizarre way of school admission: 'being kidnapped', sleeping in the cell with seasoned criminals, being remanded and appearing in court. Only criminals are handled by the police and put in cells, right?

Now and then, I tried to make sense out of the nightmare: who had orchestrated my arrest and eventual incarceration? How would they gain? Why were they talking about getting me an education when in reality I was a prisoner? If someone was so eager to educate me, why not pay for it at Kiambiriria and buy me the school uniform? How was my mother? Would I ever see her again?

Cleanliness was a real challenge because there was no water in the compound. As a result, lice had taken advantage. The disgusting pests were all over: on the blankets, on the seams of the garments and on the sleeping mats. Killing them became a hobby, but then eliminating them was impossible. They were either too many or reproduced really fast. But the real scare was scabies that mainly attacked the hands, buttocks, private parts and thighs.

Life here took on a monotonous routine. We would work the fields, also known as *fanya juu* and go for lunch before being locked up in our dormitories. My dream of going back to class was yet to materialise. Here, every staff member held the title of a teacher but none actually taught. The cook was the kitchen teacher, the watchman was the night teacher and the driver was the vehicle teacher. We were not pupils but inmates. The fantasy of a school in the city died fast. They had brought me here to rot. Kiambirira Primary School was a paradise on earth in comparison to this place. Mr. Maringa seemed more like a harmless angel. Here, fellow inmates were brutal many times over. But then there was nothing I could do to change my fate.

As aptly indicated by the name of the centre, inmates were allocated admission numbers, then admitted to various schools based on their age as well as the population in those schools. I was allocated admission number 9186. I was not the first to be snatched from my mother. 9185 boys had come before me. They had survived *fanya juu*, the lice and scabies. Two months earlier this had not occurred to me.

Christmas came. Despite our predicament, we welcomed it with all the merriment we could muster. We sang and danced to mark the big day. Some inmates acted the birth of Christ, while others recited poems. It was a special day because at ten, we had a soda with half a loaf of bread. We had rice, beans and a chunk of beef for lunch. For us, this was a big party.

# CHAPTER 5

My discharge from the centre came during the first week of January 1988. In the truck that took off at eight in the morning were seventeen boys, all about my age. Among them was Karanchu. We travelled all day. We were like sheep on their way to the slaughterhouse because no one had hinted at our destination. My mind was busy cursing the increasing distance from home. I knew Kenya was vast, but I had not imagined one could travel that long and still be within her boundaries. A section of the inmates who had been on this road before quickly volunteered as tour guides to the rest of us. However, they gave conflicting information, thereby rendering their knowledge doubtful. At one point, the issue of direction precipitated an argument and the accompanying staff had to intervene. Other guides resigned as we covered more distance, leaving just one boy named Mayaka. From the interest he attracted, it was evident he had earned some trust and respect as a guide.

"That is Lord Delamere's ranch," he said. "We are now entering Nakuru town."

The truck had four windows, thus only a few of us could see outside. By three, no one wanted to look outside. Personally, I was hungry, tired and worried that the journey would last forever. I was not the only one in misery. One boy was crying and talking in a strange language. However, some wore hardened looks, as if nothing strange was going on. Others had fallen asleep.

Finally our guide declared that we were in Kericho. Tea fields ran to the horizon. I had learnt about tea plantations in Kericho, so I readily agreed with him. I wished this was a school tour because it would have been educational and thoroughly entertaining. However, it seemed that they actually wanted to hide me in the farthest corner of the country. Why? I was as good as dead because my mother, the only person in the world who cared for me, would never trace me here.

We finally arrived at our destination. The sign at the gate screamed: Kericho Approved School. I could see some boys playing on the playfield, wearing green uniforms. They welcomed us with a chant: 'Recruits! Recruits!'

The truck came to a stop. We were called off a list as we alighted from the lorry. Here, life started on the fast track. We were allocated uniforms, a towel, tissue paper, bedding and dormitories within a record twenty minutes. Within half an hour, my towel had been stolen.

On my first Saturday, I washed one of my two uniforms and spread it on the grass outside the dormitory to dry. I went back to the dormitory only to return and find the uniform missing! I had not marked it and there was no way I could trace it. Consequently, I had to learn to survive with one shirt and one pair of shorts. I would wash the shirt and guard it to dry. Then I would tie the shirt around the waist like a skirt, wash the pair of shorts and guard it to dry. Trouble was when this exercise fell on a rainy day.

Finally, two years after being kicked out of school by Mr. Maringa, I was back in class. I was wildly excited because it was a dream come true. Eventually I had a chance to get an education. I joined standard four, just where I had left off two years before. Subjects taught in English were never interactive. This was because none of us could put words together to ask or answer a question without mixing up tenses or mispronouncing the words. Any attempt amounted to staring ridicule in the face. The teacher talked, paced, and wrote on the board. We listened, nodded in affirmation, shook our heads to refute and wrote down in our note books. When the situation presented itself, you would hear a 'yes' or 'no'. But such an answer was dangerous too because it could warrant a validation. The only voice that emanated from our mouths with confidence was laughter, which was indeed rare.

On Sundays, one of the classrooms was converted into a chapel. Usually, one of the staff members led a brief service where we sang hymns, had a Bible reading and interpretation and then prayers. Now and then, the pastor from town visited. He had a very shrewd approach to altar call. Rarely would inmates be willing to embrace salvation. Convinced that no one was ready to receive the Lord in their lives, the pastor would request us to close our eyes and bow our heads for a word of prayer. He would then ask whether anyone had a special need that he wanted God to look into. He would urge anyone in need of a miracle to raise their hands. I wanted to be home some four hundred kilometres away. I wanted to be in a proper school. I wanted a lot of miracles and my hand would go up amid a rain of thanks from the pastor.

However, instead of the pastor praying, he would then urge those with their hands in the air to take another step of faith by getting on their feet. At this juncture, everyone would be all eyes. We would then be ordered to move to the front.

"Thank you for accepting the Lord," the pastor would intone. "Your life will never be the same again. As the Bible says, 'choose eternal life and everything else shall be added unto you'." Thus, instead of receiving a miracle, I would end up being saved.

In the school, every staff member craved the title of the harshest punisher. To attain this, each one thought outside the box. Mr. Kaste's idea of physical education was to plant himself at the centre of the playing field holding a long stick and declare that he did not want to see anyone in front of him. We would cluster behind him. Then he would turn abruptly and cane anyone near him.

But the real ingenious one was Mr. Keya, a short, barrel-chested man who buttoned his shirt up to his rib cage. He was an ardent admirer of the American pugilist Mike Tyson and he would surprise you with a torrent of jabs. He happened to be my dormitory master. If at the close of the term you did not score a hundred per cent, then you were liable to as many strokes of the cane as the marks you lost.

Mr. Keya would take us to the rudimentary stage of soccer. There were three dormitories: Bomet, Towett and Tengecha. For instance, on a day when there was a football match, Mr. Keya would suddenly declare that Tengecha would be playing against Bomet. All inmates of the two dormitories would be players. That would mean about a hundred young boys chasing after the ball. Since there were no physical education kits, one team would remove their shirts to differentiate it from the other. There was no referee and, consequently, any action could be a foul, depending on how vocal and militant each team was. Sometimes, the game boiled down to blows. The losers would be caned on the soles of their feet for "torturing the ball for nothing." A draw meant trouble for the two teams. There were neither points nor a trophy for the winners, but they escaped caning.

I was a member of Towett Dormitory and on this Saturday, we were facing Tengecha Dormitory. As observed earlier, the game was so rudimentary that we allocated ourselves playing positions. The thought of scoring elated me so much that I became a striker. Since there was no offside, I simply kept the goalkeeper company waiting to get the ball and kick it past him. I was not the only opportunist. There was this classmate with a protruding forehead. He was my size and age. We got down to knowing one another as we waited for the ball to come our way.

"I miss home," the boy said yawning. "There we have lots of bananas and no hunger. I hate this place. I will never understand why it had to come to this. You see, my mother and father were always trading insults and fighting. It didn't make sense to me. They were supposed to be in love, right? One day, my father, who worked as a casual labourer with a construction company, came from work in a foul mood. He was a huge man with broad shoulders and powerful arms. He was hot-tempered. He seized my mother and strangled her to death before my eyes, then walked to the police station. To this day, I still see him do it in my sleep. During his trial, he said that my mother was sleeping with other men. He was jailed for life and I was sent here." He shook his head wearing a faraway look. "I always wonder why it had to be me. I was supposed to grow up in a home, not an approved school. I was supposed to have hope, to know that I had a future. Maybe I should have been a thief or a rapist to justify the torment I am going through here," the boy added.

"You are torturing yourself for no reason," I told him.

"Good heavens! How can you say that when you had a chance to stay out of this place and you blew it away?"

"What?" my voice was so loud he was taken aback. Our eyes locked for a long moment.

"Tell me," he asked, "what brought you here?"

I hated that question because it brought back sad memories that I never wanted to recall. But he deserved an answer. I felt a strong urge to assure him that he was not the only enemy of fate; that a good number of us were not there by choice.

"Personally, I didn't know my father. He divorced my mother before I was born because she was not educated. My mother could not pay my fees and I dropped out of school. One morning, three men in a Land Rover came home and arrested me. I was taken to court and here I am."

He looked stupefied.

"But you look like you come from a well to do family!"

"Why?"

"I don't know. Could be the way you carry yourself."

We stopped to observe a light aeroplane spraying tea fields in the distance.

"I am Alphonse Onsogo."

The ball was kicked in our direction and we dashed for it. I got it, dribbled past two opponents before someone swept me off my feet. The ball stopped at my groin and there erupted a scrum. There were feet all over my body as the players scrambled for the ball and I passed out. When I came to, Onsogo was jumping up and down shouting,

"I scored!"

Though slightly jealous, I was glad that he had saved our dormitory from the cane.

# CHAPTER 6

I sat on the grass after lunch, sunbathing. Jeremiah Wambua joined me. He was slightly shorter than me, brown-skinned and a stammerer. We were not very close but we talked now and then.

"I mm...miss home," he said conspiratorially.

"Me too," I said. "Where is home?"

"M...makueni."

I had not heard of the place before. "It must be far away."

"It... it is."

He was quiet for a while. On the road, a lorry passed, leaving a trail of dust. "Ha...have you e...ee...ever thought of e...esc...aping fro...from this p...p...place?" he asked, squirming and looking over his shoulder uncomfortably. The thought of getting back home sent my heart racing. I was twelve years old and the possibility of going through this life until I was eighteen was frightening indeed. Going back to my mother could not have improved my wellbeing, but it seemed a more welcome option. Just like Onsogo, I could not figure out a single reason why I had to undergo this torture. Fellow inmates talked of having stolen this or that or having run away from school. I had only been kicked out of school. The fact that I never made an attempt to escape made a loud statement that I was too risk averse and lacked the ingenuity to strategise an escape.

"I think everyone has."

Many inmates would have loved to be outside the walls of the school. Some even cried for being homesick.

Wambua continued squirming. "We...we... ha...ve a per...fect plan a...nd we can acco...mmo...date you."

Fleeing four hundred kilometres un-apprehended with no money seemed impossible to me.

"We ...we...ha..ve a per...fect p...p...plan," he repeated.

Curiosity seized me. What was the plan and who was involved? Why choose to accommodate me when there were so many inmates who would be interested? Was Wambua confiding in me in person or was he approaching me on behalf of other people? Was it a trap? I reflected, preparing to air the questions. However, the bell rang and we ran to class.

I didn't get a chance to enquire more about the plan that day as Wambua belonged to Bomet Dormitory. Before I slept, I fantasised on getting back home. I thought of leaving the lice, the brutality and draconian rules behind. It was a very comforting thought and I resolved to consult

Wambua on the first available opportunity the following day. I could not imagine a workable escape plan. The school was built with would-be escapees in mind. It was just one rectangle-shaped building with a wrought-iron gate. Just after the gate to the left was the dining hall which bordered the kitchen at the corner. Then there was the store, the only room with an outside door. The classrooms, four of them, were sandwiched between Towett and Tengecha dormitories. The offices, dormitory, stores, staffroom, manager and deputy's offices ran from the corner to the gate. All rooms had a ceiling and the whole building had a roof of tiles. Dormitory doors were metallic and were locked from outside. When we were in the open, there were two staff members keeping watch. They changed shifts at two o'clock on weekdays, and those on duty on Friday afternoon stayed till Monday afternoon. The green uniform was a major hindrance because it was too noticeable and there were stories of escapees being arrested and returned by members of the public.

I didn't get a chance to consult Wambua in the morning. At noon, an impromptu parade was called. We were flushed from our classes and lined up along the veranda. Word spread like bush fire that some inmates had escaped. A head count was quickly conducted and it revealed three inmates missing namely Karanchu, Malete and Wambua. It was reported that the three had been present during breakfast. A man-hunt was quickly arranged and the school Land Rover left with two staff members and a bunch of prefects. The manager gave a long speech, then we were ordered back to class. I could not concentrate as I tried to come to terms with the lost opportunity. Why, Wambua had heightened my hopes then failed to keep his promise. I could imagine him kilometres away on his way home, a possibility that infuriated me.

We were parading for lunch when the Land Rover returned. My heart almost stopped as I saw a crying Wambua being manhandled from the vehicle. He was in a floral dress. I was so relieved I had missed the opportunity to escape that I felt dizzy. To send out a warning to would be escapees, Wambua was flogged mercilessly in front of the parade. He would then be locked-up for a week in a small room called Towett 2 with just enough food to keep him alive.

In the afternoon, Mr. Keya came and stood at the door to our class. Our teacher walked outside and the two whispered for about a minute, then the teacher returned and told me to go outside. An alarm went off immediately in my mind. There was only one reason the dormitory master would want to see me: Wambua had connected me to the escape. I followed the dormitory master, silently preparing my defence. I stopped dead on entering his office. My mother was seated in a chair. She looked older and thinner but her smile was still warm and assuring. She got to her feet just as tears started streaming down her eyes. I rushed to hug her.

"I thought I had lost you," she said. "You are so thin. Are they not giving you food?" she said looking at Mr. Keya accusingly. She had a huge wooden box and she flew the lid open. It was full of ripe bananas, obviously the only item she could manage to bring me. I 'attacked' the bananas as she narrated how she had gone to Murang'a, Nairobi and finally here in search of me. Everyone else at home was fine but none was bothered about my whereabouts.

"Are you attending classes?" she asked and I nodded.

"That is good. I don't want you to end up like me. My adult education isn't much. I can write my name, but that is just about it. I always wanted you to get an education. I couldn't afford it, though. All you have to do is fight like a wounded lion and never say never."

Her words took me aback and tears started to flow down my cheeks. Didn't she know how irritating the lice and scabies were? Did she know the mental torture of donning the green uniform? What about the caning and bullying?

"This is not how I would have wanted it, but it seems the only way. You are my only love and I will always be there for you. Think of me as the star in the skies. I will always be watching over you."

The bananas were too many and so I invited my friends to share. Two hours later, my mother left for home.

Two days later, Malete arrived in the company of a policeman. He too was caned and locked up. The week-long punishment took its toll on the two escapees and they lost weight, confidence and buoyancy. Malete narrated his story a day after completing his week-long punishment.

"During break time, we edged to the fence where Karanchu had made a cave of some sort. He had made enough room in the cypress fence to hold the three of us."

"When did he cut the fence?" I ventured.

"He said he had taken two weeks when we were playing," Malete said. "He had three dresses and headscarves ready for the journey. We changed and emerged from the other side of the fence. We actually ran into that cook, Madam Akoth. She didn't recognise us. Once in town, Karanchu told Wambua to wait in the public toilet. Karanchu and I walked into one of the Nairobi-bound buses. Karanchu told me to slip under the seat and he then left for Wambua. We were to regroup in Nakuru. When I reached Nakuru, I emerged from under the seat unnoticed. I walked to the door and saw this policeman looking at me curiously. Well, he arrested me."

Two weeks later, Karanchu arrived in the company of two policemen. He had been arrested in Kisumu after snatching a wristwatch. As was the norm, he began his week-long stay in Towett 2.

That evening Malete was fuming like a wounded buffalo.

"The rascal! The Devil incarnate! We were not meant to go anywhere. He had other plans. He left Wambua at the public toilet knowing that he would be apprehended within town. Wambua would give us away. Police stations along Kericho-Nairobi route would be notified of our escape. That is why when I got to Nakuru, a policeman was waiting for me. But Karanchu was nowhere to be seen; he had taken a bus to Kisumu. He had used us."

"Ingenious!" someone exclaimed.

# CHAPTER 7

It seemed to me it rained every day in the afternoon. On this Saturday, it appeared the rain would be falling early. Since his week-long stay in Towett 2, Wambua had kept to himself. Presently, he sat on the veranda and I joined him. He was sharpening a metal blade about six inches long and an inch wide.

"Are you planning to peel potatoes?" I ventured.

He looked at me long and hard, then shook his head. "Ki…kill some…someone."

I chuckled. "Hopefully, I am not the doomed one."

"Do… you k…know why I was ad…ad…mitted?"

"You ran from school or something."

He was silent for a long moment. "I k…killed so… some…one."

"That is not funny."

"I… I am se…rious." I turned to face him sharply. Indeed, he looked dead serious. He told me of the class bully in his former school who used to make jokes at him because he was a stammerer. Whenever he reported him, the bully would waylay him on his way home and beat him up. He would report him the following day and in the evening the punishment would recur. Eventually, Wambua realised, to his uttermost dismay, that reporting him did more harm than good. His father's attempt to intervene proved futile. While his father was a peasant farmer, his foe's father was a local business magnate. Wambua loved school but the environment was unbearable. He decided to arm himself. He took a discarded knife at home and sharpened it. He always carried it in his bag. One day, as the bully stepped in front of the class for his round of jokes, Wambua confronted him holding the knife and told him enough was enough. The bully was too sure of himself and he attempted to disarm him. Wambua stabbed him in the chest and he died on the way to hospital.

I was quiet for a long moment as I digested what I had just heard. I knew some of the inmates had done terrible things—but murder! Personally, I had been subjected to ridicule and knew how demeaning it could be. Wambua had clearly undergone worse times, but murder was too much of a solution.

The trouble is, he was bent on doing it again. Looking at him, I could not underrate his resolve. I found myself thinking of possible candidates. This however was not easy because if it was a bully, the place was littered with enough of them. Then Karanchu came to mind. According to Malete, Karanchu had used them.

"Someone is beating you up?" I ventured but Wambua continued to sharpen the blade.

"Worse. H...he is us...ing me as h...his wife."

It took him some effort to say that and he wiped a tear off his face. Now that was a big problem. That homosexual activities were rampant was an open secret. I had first witnessed the bizarre activity in Murang'a Remand Home where one boy had the audacity to approach me. Generally, bigger inmates molested younger ones. Some abused fellow inmates to settle scores. Some cases surfaced with the victim becoming a laughing-stock and the abuser a conqueror. Then the story decorated toilet walls and it was left to the victim to obliterate them. Receiving a beating was no big deal; it was being abused while asleep that caused the shivers.

Wambua said that this inmate had been abusing him for weeks now. He suffered silently, to avoid humiliation. He was unwilling to give a name. However, from his description, the abuser was overwhelming; older, bigger – a real nightmare. He strongly believed the administration could not help. When Karanchu came up with the escape plan, he had jumped at it, eager to get away from it all. Well, the escape had failed and he was back in hell.

"I f...feel so d...dirty."

"Who is it?" I pressed.

"Y...you wi...ll know on...ce he is d...dead."

"You won't get away with a second murder."

"W...what wo...uld you do?"

That was the all-important question that kept me awake at night. I wished I had the answer. All I knew was that I could not resort to murder. But Wambua was not interested in what I could not do, but in a solution.

The rain started pouring and we had to take cover. I was seriously disturbed because I was privy to an impending tragedy but could not avert it. I could not warn the administration that a murder was about to take place because I only had Wambua's word for it and if faced with accusations, he would definitely deny them. I went to sleep every night trying to picture a possible victim and woke up in the morning expecting sad news of a dead inmate. This went on for a week and I hoped Wambua had changed his mind. Then one day just before we went to sleep, a sharp cry cut the air. Someone was crying out in anguish, his mournful wails almost swallowed by a number of concerned voices shouting for help. The noise was coming from Bomet Dormitory and my heart started racing. I pictured an inmate bleeding to death.

"What was happening at night?" I asked Geoffrey, a resident of Bomet the following morning.

"It is Willy."

"Willy the captain?" Geoffrey nodded. "What about him?"

He smiled, and I wondered what sort of a sadist he was. Someone was dead and he was smiling! "His thing was bitten by an insect."

"His thing?"

He touched his fly. "It is the size of your head. You better take care of yours," he said and walked off. I was thoughtful for a long moment. I strongly believed that the whole incident had everything to do with Wambua. If so, then Wambua found himself been between a rock and a hard place. The captain was no ordinary inmate; he was above the law, a small god. You could not fight him either, even if you were as big and energetic because he was always in the company of some disciples. You could not just walk to the housekeeper and tell him that the school captain was sexually molesting you. You suffered silently.

Later on, I caught up with Wambua. He was sharpening the metal blade.

"It wasn't an insect, was it?"

From his pocket Wambua produced red pepper.

"Wow! You mean..." I started. "That was ingenious! Who gave you the idea?"

He tapped his head with his index finger.

"T...that w...was a warn...ing. If...If he d...doesn't heed then I k...kill him."

The captain heeded this warning and with time, Wambua quit sharpening his weapon. The story that an insect had bitten the captain remained because by refuting it, Wambua would have been forced to admit to being molested sexually, which meant humiliation.

# CHAPTER 8

It had become clear now that I was in the institution to stay. My mother loved me unequivocally, but thought it better for me to stay put. "Fight like a wounded lion," she had said. In effect, I was not welcome back home. This was my battlefield, my home, and the best course of action was to adapt to the environment.

Somehow, having broken the law seemed heroic, whereas the opposite sounded naïve. One was either a hero or an amateur based on the cause for incarceration. Being green made one an easy prey. To avoid giving myself away, I resolved to keep my affairs to myself. Neither would I lie nor would I tell the truth. Being in the midst of street-wise boys, I quickly learnt and polished my Sheng. The boys from the streets were only too eager to share their exploits, thus I was able to learn about street activities.

Four months down the road, I had learnt to see the brighter side of life. I had gone through two years of hopelessness, but I was back in class eventually. The environment was far from conducive, but I was learning. We were allowed to post letters once a month. All that one had to do was write the letter and give it to the dormitory master for approval and posting. I wrote to my mother every month, addressing the letters through my former primary school, but received no response. Probably, the letters didn't go past the dormitory master. Again, my mother was illiterate. Nevertheless by writing, I felt I had fulfilled an important responsibility.

After six months, one qualified for an outing, commonly known as *runju*. I never really came to know the administration's rationale for *runju*. Recreation was the word they used, but we took it as a chance to beg and scavenge. We begged in the streets of the town and if one was not lucky enough, we passed by the dump site looking for something edible. On Sunday, immediately after lunch, we paraded in twos for inspection. To qualify for *runju*, you had to be disciplined and smart. For you to be smart, you simply washed your khaki shorts and shirt and ironed them by placing them under the mattress overnight. The face of anyone who seriously wanted to go for *runju* would be gleaming against the afternoon sun. This is because with time, one learnt the art of harvesting top layer from soup in a small bottle. Then you used it like normal body lotion. The main problem was its expiry date. You smelt like rotten food if you applied it after two days.

We left for town at one in groups of five and returned at five. Once we got out of the gate, we went our different ways with plans to regroup on our way back.

My first outing was an adventure. I had never been to a big town on my own with nothing else to do but loiter. Onsogo had become a close friend and we stuck together.

On this day, we were not lucky. We were expected back at five and it was already four, so we rushed to the dump site. Luck was on our side because a pick-up from Tea Hotel had just completed off-loading its waste. We promptly attacked our new-found treasure. The dump site was surrounded by tall trees inhabited by monkeys that relied a lot on the dump site for their survival. Thus, they were happy to see the pick-up. However, we interrupted their party and they were not happy about it. They were closing in on us from all sides. I alerted Onsogo who was lost skinning a chicken leg.

"We fight them," he said. He picked a nearby stick but before he could raise it, two bottles crushed above our heads. The monkeys laughed and charged towards us. Cornered, we were forced to leave the dump site through a forest trail. There were stories about man-eaters who lived in the forest, so you can understand my apprehension as we walked. At the edge of the forest, we saw a man burying something. Onsogo suggested that we bolt but I told him to lie low. My heart was beating loudly and I was sweating profusely. I had never come this close to death. Satisfied, the man collected his implements and left. We debated for quite a while whether or not to uncover his secret.

"We should leave," I said.

"Maybe he was burying money," Onsogo said.

"What?" Before I could stop him he was standing on the fresh soil. He took a stick and started digging. Whatever the man had buried wasn't far and Onsogo's stick hit against plastic. He removed soil to uncover a jerrican. Holding it by the handle we pulled it from its shallow grave. Onsogo opened the lid, decanted a little of the liquid inside and tasted it. "Sweet as honey," I said.

"It is *busaa*," Onsogo said. "It takes three days after brewing to ferment. They hide it in the fields to avoid being arrested."

Faced with the problem of containers to serve the liquid, we imbibed it in turns direct from the jerrican. When our stomachs could take no more, we carried the remainder and hid it in the school fence. I went to check on it the following day and I found it missing. I accosted Onsogo demanding to know whether he had moved it, but he denied flatly. Then, two days, later in the afternoon, Onsogo started singing in Ekegusii in class. This was bizarre considering that the mathematics teacher was in class. The teacher shouted at him to shut up, but instead, Onsogo got to his feet and started to dance. He was weak on his feet and he swayed, then landed on the floor.

The day turned out to be one of my worst in the school. Evidently, Onsogo had moved the *busaa* and lied to me. In his selfishness, he wanted to use it for a longer period. With time the *busaa* had matured so when he took it after lunch he got drunk. I was so mad with him because in his drunkenness, he had mentioned my name adversely, earning me punishment. We had to be caned, made to slash grass round the building and miss *runju* for four consecutive weeks.

"I am so sorry I lied to you," Onsogo said as we were slashing. "Look, even if I had not moved it the two of us would have been drunk, which changes nothing."

"No!" I protested. "We would have finished it before it matured."

At this point, my friend admitted his guilt. To show that he was really sorry, he promised to give me his piece of meat that day. This was a moving gesture, and we became friends again.

# CHAPTER 9

On this Sunday, we had gone round and round in town like birds that had lost their point of reference. We decided to rest near the bus station. Huge buses fascinated me and I could watch them for hours. In terms of begging, it had not been a lucky day so far. Then, out of the blue, this woman walked to us and gave us ten shillings. Back in those day, ten shillings had real purchasing power. Bubbling over with gusto, we thanked her profusely then embarked on budgeting for our windfall. I needed to buy a fountain pen and I suggested we split the cash.

"That is perfect with me," Onsogo intoned.

Just then Mbiru joined us. He was older in the school and slightly bigger than us.

"Guys," he said in merriment. "This is my lucky day! Come I buy you something to eat."

We had no words to express our joy. We exchanged glances then followed Mbiru into a nearby hotel. Mbiru ordered *ugali mboga* for each one of us.

The waiter looked at us suspiciously. "You have money?"

"Of course!" Mbiru said impatiently. "If we didn't, we would have said, 'please give us something to eat.' We didn't say that, did we? We buy when we can, we beg when we can't buy." Mbiru laughed and we joined in the laughter. Assured, the waiter went for our order.

"I love *runju*," Mbiru was saying. "It gives me a chance to fill my big stomach."

"The problem is the quantity of food they give us," I protested.

Our order was brought. We were famished and talking ceased immediately as we concentrated on devouring the food. By the time I was halfway done, Mbiru was through. He poured water into a glass and drank it in one big gulp. He then leaned back on his chair and belched.

"Oh, my big stomach," he said. "It is half full. I think I should have a second helping. It is one of those rare days, you know. But first a visit to the toilet." He got to his feet and walked towards the hotel toilets.

By the time we were done, Mbiru had not returned. We could not leave because he had not settled the bill. The waiter came for his money. We told him the person responsible for settling the bill was in the toilet.

"Toilet?" he asked. "What toilet? We don't have toilets in this hotel. That is a way out."

That settled it. We had been swindled. We were forced to pay with our money.

We caught up with Mbiru the following day. He was not the type to be rattled easily, at least not by someone like me or Onsogo. He kept cool and even smiled as we ranted and raved. After hurling several insults, Onsogo took off hurriedly. I stood there studying Mbiru with the helplessness of a boxer dying to teach his opponent a lesson but painfully aware he lacks what it takes to do so. My opponent was taller and more energetic. Well, David triumphed, but Goliath is always the best bet.

"You are angry with me," Mbiru said finally. "You are not like Onsogo. You know, you make me feel guilty. Well, I will make it up to you. See me on Sunday."

On the following Sunday, when we were leaving for *runju,* I called Mbiru aside.

"You owe me something, remember?"

"Sure. Do you want to eat bread?" he asked.

I nodded vigorously.

"Good. Then a loaf of bread you will eat. Better still I can teach you how to get a loaf of bread."

Mbiru was getting more captivating and I took huge strides to keep pace.

"For you to get what you want just study people's routine, right? You know why I got you that day so clean? I knew you love free things, no offence intended. Well, you want a loaf of bread? Here is the catch. Every teacher buys goods on credit and pays for them at end month.

Do you follow? Mr. Keya buys his from that shop. All you have to do is this."

I could not believe my ears. Mbiru had conned me and, in repayment, was teaching me to steal.

"That is outrageous!" I exclaimed. "Are you sick? Mr. Keya is the worst…"

"Exactly why no one, himself included, would expect anyone to lie using his name," he said. "Listen, to the shopkeeper a loaf of bread is a bridge to riches. To you it is a lifesaver. You are not stealing."

"I must be out of my mind to be listening to you."

I looked at the shop where Mr. Keya apparently bought things on credit. I imagined having a loaf of bread and my heart started racing. I looked at the piece of paper in my hand bearing my dormitory master's faked signature.

"What if I am caught?"

"Not unless you give yourself away. Go."

I breathed in hard, fought to ignore the sweat dripping under my armpits, and started towards the shop. My heart was beating hard against my rib cage. There were two other shoppers and I handed the piece of paper to the shopkeeper. He looked at it hard and long. I stood there fearing the worst, my heart threatening to stop. I was about to take off when he reached for a loaf of bread and steel wool and handed them to me. Untold relief swept over me. I started off fighting the urge to bolt.

That would be giving myself away, I told myself striving to act normal.

"Congratulations!" Mbiru said.

"You made me lie," I accosted him once we were out of the shop's vicinity.

"Relax, will you? You were perfect." He divided the loaf in two and handed me my share. We started our journey to town.

"What about this?" I asked holding the steel wool. Mbiru took it and flung it to the bush. "Who would expect you to lie to get steel wool? Oh, we should have included a packet of milk. Anyway, a loaf of bread is better than nothing."

Our conversation was suspended as we ate the loaf. Mbiru finished long before I was halfway through.

"I once had lunch at the Hilton," Mbiru said. "You know, the rich have this peculiar attitude. To them cost is not an issue; they can easily spend on you. But they consider you a nuisance. So on this day, I waited outside the big hotel and this man pulled up. I accompanied him inside and occupied a table next to his. When the waiter approached me, I whispered, 'I am with him. He hates being disturbed. I will eat anything.' The waiter turned to the man who smiled. He brought me a lot of food. Don't ask me what it was. I ate fast and walked out."

I had witnessed Mbiru's prowess as a con artist, but the Hilton part sounded too sensational to be true.

"Oh, my big stomach!" he said. "I need some milk."

We were in town and I was afraid he would suggest I lie again. I waited patiently ready to refuse. Then something happened. Mbiru started shaking all over like a leaf. Thinking he was trying to act funny, I was about to laugh when his mouth started foaming. In a split second, his eyes opened wide and only the whites were visible.

"Are you okay?" I asked. Before I could reach him he collapsed to the ground. Some pedestrians surrounded him.

"He needs milk," I said, remembering Mbiru's words. Someone ran off and returned with a packet of milk. We supported Mbiru to a sitting position so that he could take the milk. After several sips he stopped shaking. The good Samaritans deposited him under a shade then moved on.

"That is enough. You can have the rest," he said.

"What? You are the one who is sick!" I said.

"Sick?" Mbiru asked chuckling. "I just faked it. You know, we are all always ready to rescue a dying person. You have your loaf of bread and a bonus packet of milk." He stood and walked off.

There were many boys with skills like Mbiru who were willing to share them. The street-wise, self-styled teachers were more appealing than real ones and had a lot of followers. While real teachers taught us how to face the future, the street-wise ones gave survival skills; glue-sniffing and petrol-sniffing to fight reality, playing *kamali* and cards to earn what one did not have and draughts and *mbao* to kill time. We did not have money to play cards, but we bid the highest stakes: food.

It was a whole new world.

# Chapter 10

As I celebrated Christmas of 1989, the second one in Kericho, I knew my stay in the school was coming to an end. Come January the following year, I would join standard six. The school offered tuition up to standard five. I could not be accommodated anymore. My analysis was correct because, early in January, my name was among a number of inmates who would be going on transfer. Indeed, all my classmates were on the list.

Transfers were dreaded because they meant facing the unknown. Kingpins lost their clout. One was separated from his friends. It meant bullying. During my two year stay, I had won so much confidence among staff members as a disciplined inmate that Mr. Keya had appointed me the dormitory prefect. It was not easy to leave all these.

We were supposed to hand over our textbooks, bedding and uniform, an exercise that lasted until eleven. We left at noon. Our journey was a dull one. Immediately after Kericho town it started raining heavily and we had to slow down. I had wrestled my way to one of the windows for a better view of the country, but it turned out to be a disappointment when darkness blanketed the earth. I was not sure where I was being taken, and I was eager to know how I got there.

We arrived at Dagoretti in the wee hours of the morning. I was cold, sleepy and hungry. The truck had been stuck twice in the mud and we had been forced to push it. Here, twelve names of those who would be remaining were read out. I was not one of them and so we continued with our journey.

I must have slept for several hours because when I woke up, the truck was at a standstill and everyone was milling out. It was ten o'clock and we were in Othaya. This realisation lifted my spirit because I was closer home.

Here, someone with religious inclination had named the dormitories. There was St. Peter's, St. John's, St. Paul's and St. Mark's. I was quite small compared to other boys and I became a resident of St. Peter's Junior. The dormitories were old and oblong-shaped. A protrusion that housed the toilet had been added.

The aura in the school was academic. It was a full-fledged primary school that ran from standard one through standard eight. I had finally succeeded in my endeavour to adapt because life here was more bearable.

Just like Kericho, there was only one cook on duty at a time. Thus, there was a kitchen and dining hall duty roster that rotated round the dormitories on a weekly basis. Being on duty was something to die for because it meant filling one's belly. To survive in the kitchen, one had to exploit every possible opportunity. With time, one learnt how to swallow hot ugali without chewing. If one was on duty, they could trade their usual ration for things like biro pens, stop watches or give ugali, githeri or rice in exchange for beef. One could give it to a bully of their choice for protection. Better still, one could give it to their dormitory prefect to ensure that they always represented their dormitory in the kitchen.

Othaya was the home of *wandindi*, a musical instrument made from a tin, a piece of hide, a stick and wire. Rudimentary as it was, it produced heavenly melodies in the hands of an expert. It was an integral item among the few assets one was allowed to own.

On Saturday afternoon, we went for general cleaning at the nearby river. Now and then, inmates staged a swimming contest. The rest of us lined up along the banks of the river to cheer the contestants. There was a straight stretch of about fifty metres beyond which the river had a fall. I was eight years when I decided I would never swim again. It had occurred in a very dramatic fashion. There happened to be no big rivers near home where one could swim. We therefore blocked the flow of the seasonal stream nearby to make a dam, something that usually brought a lot of acrimony from fellow users down-stream. On this day, I dived, only to see a black mamba in the water. I was already airborne and efforts to control my fall proved futile. If bravery was judged by coming into contact with a serpent, then I failed the test because my bowels emptied before I crashed against it.

However, after watching the contestants fight it out on several occasions, I fell in love with swimming all over again and rescinded my earlier decision. Indeed, I endeavoured to be the champion one day. I had a long way to go because it dawned on me that we never actually swam back at home, we only dived and played with water. To be the winner, I required some serious practice. I therefore looked forward to Saturday afternoons eagerly. Sharing my sentiments was Onsogo. We became so zealous we decided to create more time for the practice. We would go to the river after classes when other inmates were in the playing field. This went on for several days until one day hell broke loose.

We were busy practising backstroke when Abdi, the reigning champion, appeared. Having been born and brought up at the coast, he swam like a fish and it was almost impossible to beat him. His visit was a rare treat because he offered to coach us. According to him, the first step in mastering swimming was the ability to hold one's breath for the longest time possible. He was the champion and his advice was gospel to our ears. Thus when he told us to dive and stay under as long as possible, we filled our lungs with oxygen and dived at the count of three.

I surfaced after what seemed like an eternity then froze.

Onsogo surfaced a moment later. Abdi was nowhere to be seen. We usually put on two pairs of shorts so that we could use the inner one to swim. Our dry clothes were missing too.

We had been duped.

Just then, the bell for supper rang. In our swimming bliss, we had lost count of time. The general rule was that if one was late for parade by five minutes, they missed the meal. During the day, the dormitories were always locked so we could not get clothes to change. We had been caught between a rock and a very hard place. After exploring our options, we decided to attend the parade. Failure to appear was too risky because it could be interpreted to mean that we had escaped. With luck, we could get away with caning.

We arrived thus, half naked and dripping with water amid mocking laughter. We had taken our chances, but we were unlucky because we got punished and missed supper.

# CHAPTER 11

Being in a multi-ethnic society, no one laughed at me for using my mother's name. Nevertheless, the fact that I wasn't baptized still bothered me a lot. The mockery at Kiambiriria Primary School still echoed in my ears, underscoring the importance of a baptismal name. On Wednesday, we attended a pastoral programme in the morning where we learnt catechism. On Sundays, we went to a Roman Catholic Church in town where an Italian priest impressively said mass in Gikuyu. On this Sunday, I felt as though the Father was talking to me personally.

"We want God to give us exactly what we ask for and within our time. God is not a respecter of men. If you ask for a car, God can give you good health so that you can work to attain your wish. You want a good meal, a good house, a beautiful wife; God has given you a chance to get an education so that you may acquire these one day. However, things don't just happen. When Jesus turned water into wine at a wedding in the Cana of Galilee, He ordered the servants to fill the containers with water. He could have done this. When he fed a multitude he asked his disciples, 'How many loaves do you have?' God is ready to perform a miracle in your life. But you have a part to play to realise your miracle."

The message hit home perfectly. I had longed to have an education so badly I had lied for it. I had longed to speak English. I had thirsted for a bright future. Here was the chance! Amid all the tribulations was a miracle unfolding. But I needed to play my part to realise the miracle; to work hard, to be disciplined, and to be thankful for my blessings.

A surprise was waiting for me back at school. On arrival, I was summoned to the manager's office. I had never been to the manager's office before. My mind went into high gear as I tried to fathom why the manager would want to see me. Assuring myself that it was a mistake I ran to the door, knocked and upon a 'come in' I pushed the door open, entered, then I stopped dead. Seated in the office were my grandmother, my uncle and, of course, the manager. I stood rooted at the door as I tried to guess what was cooking.

"Please have a seat," the manager said and I occupied a chair. "You know these people?" I nodded. I had not seen the duo for two long years. Even then, we had lived in two different worlds. What had changed that they should pay me a visit? Where was my mother?

I was more intrigued when the manager ordered for sodas. He was generally a formal man and his attempt to play a generous host seemed strange.

"It is a big day," he declared but his voice didn't carry the sentiment. "You never had visitors before, I gather."

I nodded. I turned to look at my visitors who smiled reassuringly. We lapsed into a disturbing silence for a long moment.

"You are a good boy," the manager said awkwardly. "Your visitors here share my sentiments."

That was a fat lie. How could they know?

"You went to church today?"

I nodded. "Good. Then you know that God created us and with time, we go to heaven to live with Him." He stopped to choose his words. "It concerns your mother. I am sorry to inform you that she has passed on. I am very sorry."

I sat there fighting the urge to wail. Admittedly, the manager had striven to be gentle in breaking the news, but nothing could be comforting. Someone was dead and it was my mother, the only person on earth who really cared, and words could not change the fact. Tears blurred my vision and I fought them back. I did not want to break down in front of these strangers. I prayed for a distraction, a haven to rescue me from the inhuman torment of the moment. But the loss was so tragic, so consuming and cruel that nothing could be more arresting. I forced my mind to focus on happier days in the past, finally settling on my last encounter with my mother. That was two years before, in Kericho. I recalled eating bananas to my full and sharing them out with friends. That was love beyond words, something that denoted the extent of my loss.

"You are my only love and I will always be there for you," her last words came to me.

"The Lord loved her more than we did and that is why He took her," my uncle was saying.

'Think of me as the star in the skies. I will always be watching over you,' my mother had promised.

"This is a difficult time for all of us," Grandma intoned. They didn't want to burden me with grief so they had already buried her.

"You are welcome home. We will take care of you."

Never quit!

"Before she left us she knit a sweater for you," my grandmother said, ruffling a piece of polythene paper to produce a green pullover. It was heavy and meant to last. Only my mother could have done it so perfectly. They urged me to try it on, something I found utterly ridiculous given the circumstances.

Fare thee well, Mum.

Finally, to my utter relief, the two left.

The first reaction to my grandmother's invitation was refusal. It was paradoxical, really, that her own daughter was not welcome home but her grandson was. Was she sympathetic or remorseful? What had changed now that my mother was dead? According to them, my mother had been incurably inhospitable. To me, she was sidelined and, like every living thing with an ego, she did what she had to do to survive.

The old question was yet to be answered: who had engineered my arrest and why?

As days went by, curiosity seized me. I had not been home for two long years. How would it feel to be out there? How would it feel to be out of the uniform, without someone watching over you, mingling with the public, roving freely? How was everyone doing? How was beautiful Anastasia?

# CHAPTER 12

As the end of first term drew near, I grew more excited at the prospect of going home. I knew it depicted some weakness on my part, even lack of ideals, but yes, I would be going there. Not that it was much of a home. But then, I needed somewhere to go, somewhere to belong. I needed some people to identify with.

I imagined a myriad of things. I imagined meeting Anastasia and talking to her. I imagined narrating stories to a huge audience; about the night runners of Kisii; about the fighting bhang-stuffed bulls of Luhyaland. I had seen the world: Nairobi, Nakuru, Kericho. I had met people from most tribes of Kenya. I felt like a war hero on his way home from the battlefield. Worries, bitterness and the fact that I was an inmate took the backseat.

On the eve of the big day, I hardly slept. I could hardly wait to be home. Instead of bus fare, we were given travel permits. These were vouchers offered at a premium redeemable at the Department of Children's Services offices. Trouble was getting someone to accept them.

After a troublesome journey that took all day, I arrived in my home village of Kiambirira. I smelt trouble at once.

There is a way people communicate with their eyes. They could be tight-lipped, but you still get the message loud and clear. Wherever I passed, people would stop and stare. The message hit home loud and clear: it was all about the green uniform. It was a brutal wake-up call that I was not a war hero – at least not to these people – but an inmate. The adage that some prisons don't have walls became a rude reality to me.

A lot had changed at home. Our mud-walled house had been pulled down and a timber one built. It had two rooms: my room and my grandmother's kitchen. They said it belonged to me, something I found awkward. To start with, to get to my room, I had to pass through my grandmother's kitchen. Thus I had to wake up early to open the front door for her. Secondly, she cooked using firewood, thereby smoking me out of my abode. Anything white turned to a dull colour in a matter of days. Thirdly, one's house is where one has some privacy and I had none.

Everyone seemed to have changed; they had either grown taller or older. One of my uncles had another child who was struggling to pronounce my name.

The audience for my stories remained a fantasy. Instead, I was faced with a suspicious society that asked degrading questions. "Is it true that you are caned during breakfast, lunch and supper? Why were you taken to Wamumu?" Wamumu was the approved school closest to my home. It was infamous for all the wrong reasons.

Parents would warn their notorious children that, failing to behave, they risked being sent to Wamumu.

Whenever I joined a group of playing children they would lose interest in the game and leave one after the other. I fought to convince myself that I was imagining things but it was happening before my own eyes. However, they could not resist my *wandindi*. I was an expert on the instrument, and my audience was always left asking for more.

One day, a middle-aged man approached me, bragging about having been an inmate. He hailed from the neighbourhood and had a bad reputation.

"I am one of the pioneers," he said importantly. "Those were the days. You have heard of Wang'iu, no? That is me. I escaped three times. By the time I was through, they were just too happy to let me go. I was a nightmare to them. Is Majira still there? We once beat him up, Kabangi and I."

Kabangi, the man in the cell! The man who had threatened to kill a policeman.

"You need something in your pocket to survive that hell-hole. Imagine going without a cigarette for a whole day! As a comrade, I am obliged to lend a hand. I will show you how to get money around this place. Look, there is this mission we have with Kabangi. It will be on the night of the 14th...."

74

"Look, I must run. Can we talk about this later please?"

"Sure. You know where to find me?"

"I do."

As I was leaving, I saw Patrick's father – my uncle who had visited me in Othaya – looking at me.

My fantasy for an easy time remained just that, because we were always working. There the cow to graze, fields to weed and other menial chores to take care of.

At home I was a stranger. My relatives treated me with caution. Phobia was mirrored in their eyes. I was home two years before and even then our relationship had not been cordial. I could hardly complain because, as it were, I had come here because I needed somewhere to go but had no other choice. I was yet to know what prompted them to invite me back. I didn't know whether to interpret it as remorse or pity. Ice between us was broken by a misfortune. I always went to bed early and by ten I would be fast asleep. On this Monday, I was awakened by commotion outside. I walked to the window and opened it slightly. I could see shadowy figures moving aimlessly. I dressed up quickly and went outside.

"What is it?" I asked Patrick, who was one of my cousins. We were age-mates but he appeared physically bigger. He had taken after his father, who was a big man. But then a better diet could have made the difference. He was in standard eight, two classes ahead of me because I had lost two years. A favourite with girls, he was always chasing after fashion trends and I had seen him wearing an earring.

"There is an owl," he said. "It is hooting and Papa is positive someone will die. You know what? That is nonsense. I should be dead asleep, you know. He shouldn't have woken me up."

He was so emotional he had a problem wording his bitterness. The owl was on a huge blue gum on the neighbouring farm. It was a pitch-dark night and the only course of action was to throw stones up the tree hoping to scare the bird away. This was an uphill task considering the darkness and the height of the tree. Patrick's mother held a lantern above her head which lost the battle to lighten up the dark night. Patrick's father had a makeshift sling and was swinging it over his head ready to fire. He let go one side and the piece of stone flew into the night. We waited for a report but none was forthcoming. Obviously, there was no telling what direction the missile had taken.

"Good grief!" Patrick muttered.

His father released another stone that whizzed into the night. The sound of a mooing cow made us start. Patrick's father picked the lantern and we all followed him. His cow lay on the ground, writhing. The stone had caught it square on its forehead. It kicked hard then went still.

The old man turned. His face was a death mask.

"I will be damned!" Patrick exclaimed silently. His voice had faltered. "Could it be true? But then he has no experience with the sling."

"Satan," it was Patrick's mother. "I condemn you in the name of Jesus Christ. I am ordering you to leave us in peace. We refuse the spirit of death in the mighty name of Jesus!" she carried on.

It was eleven in the night. Patrick's father swore that one way or the other the owl had to leave. He declared that he had the perfect plan of making sure it went away and never returned. This was by putting two nails on the stem of the blue gum. But the tree was in the middle of thorny bushes which meant clearing them first. He dashed to the house and returned with clearing implements.

"This is going to be a long night," Patrick complained. He picked a machete and we started clearing the bushes.

# CHAPTER 13

The holiday finally came to an end and everyone bid me goodbye, guardedly. It was clear I had failed to live up to their expectations in many ways. I had read malice in their zeal to know about me and my school. No answer could attract any empathy, but instead made a juicier bedside story. I had therefore divulged as little as I could, only allowing my *wandindi* to communicate freely.

I was leaving when Patrick's father called me aside. "I must confess that I was a little apprehensive when I allowed you back," he started. Judging from his look, he had carefully planned and timed this encounter. "But for that talk with Wang'iu, you have proved my worries unfounded. He has a bad history, you know. He was an inmate, just like you. What were you talking about?"

Patrick's father would have had a field day if he knew about Wang'iu's attempt to induct me into his gang. I didn't want to lie but I could not divulge the particulars of our encounter.

"Nothing important," I said.

He looked at me for a long moment then said: "I won't press but if I see you with him again, I won't allow you in this compound again."

We studied each other for a long, uncomfortable moment. I had for so long nursed the inkling that he had orchestrated my arrest and eventual incarceration. He singularly had made my mother's life unbearable. There were so many nasty things I wanted to tell him but I managed to control myself. I only asked the question that had troubled my soul for weeks now.

"Exactly why did you invite me back?"

"Did you have somewhere else to go?" he asked. His voice was hard. I must confess that his question was valid and innocent. However, owing to my circumstances, I interpreted it differently. Did he mean he had invited me back simply because I had nowhere else to go? Didn't I belong? I was on the verge of tears and I didn't want him to see me cry. I started towards the gate promising myself never to return.

I had very little luggage: my *wandindi* and a small metallic box said to have belonged to my grandfather. Inside were two boiled cobs of maize, a boiled egg that Patrick's mother had given me and a fountain pen. The box was not necessarily for carrying things but for storage back in school. For the first time in my life, I was the proud owner of underpants and a pair of rubber shoes, thanks to my aunt Mercy.

On my way to town, I saw Anastasia in the company of two girls. She was big and her beauty seemed to glow. She stopped long enough to look at me. In her eyes, I read recognition, something that made my heart race and sweat to ooze from every pore on my skin. Somehow, I didn't feel confident to talk to her.

The journey from home to school could take two hours. However, I left home early and took my time touring the towns on the way before I boarded a minibus to Nyeri. When the conductor came upon me, I produced the travel permit and handed it to him. His face darkened.

"Good grief!" he exclaimed more in amusement than annoyance. "I ask for bus fare and you hand me a donation list!"

"It is not a donation list."

His face hardened. "Then what is it?"

I was now sure he could not read.

"A travel permit."

"What?"

My uniform caught his eye, thereby changing his attitude instantly. He handed me the permit with his left hand while his right rushed to his hip pocket in reflex. Satisfied that the contents of his pocket were secure, he moved on. Other passengers started looking at me strangely.

I arrived in Nyeri at eleven o'clock; too early to board another vehicle to Othaya, hence I decided to tour the town. I had roamed the town for about an hour, when I came upon a group of people surrounding an acrobatic troupe. I decided to squeeze my way to the front for a better view. As the crowd grew, there was constant pushing and shoving.

"Beware of pick-pockets," someone warned. The man on my right thrust his hand in his pocket then jolted as if he had received an electric shock. "My money!" he howled. He looked around, his eyes finally resting on me. "Hey, young thief, I need it back."

Suddenly the audience lost interest in the troupe and accosted me. Someone snatched my box while another one slapped me hard across the face. A gunshot invaded the mid-morning air and everyone fell on their belly.

I found myself facing a policeman.

"Where is it?"

"I didn't steal anything. I am on my way back to school." He frisked me. Satisfied, he escorted me to the bus stop.

"Do you know what that uniform means to these people? 'Guilty as charged.' I hate collecting charred bodies. Take your bus and get lost."

# CHAPTER 14

I can vividly recall that in standard seven, we studied mathematics up to page fourteen. After that, we had no teacher and, to our ignorant minds, this was good riddance because mathematics was an unnecessary nuisance. By the time we joined standard eight, the highest score stood at thirty per cent. It is against this background that Mr. Sospeter Oketch, nicknamed Mr. Sapiens Sapiens, stepped in as our mathematics teacher. He once gave us a problem in algebra and pledged a hundred shillings to the person who got it right. No one did. He solved it, bragged about the level of his IQ, asserting that he was not a Homo Sapiens but Homo Sapiens Sapiens, and so Mr. Sapiens Sapiens he became. He was the Deputy Manager and he had only volunteered to teach us.

Mr. Sapiens Sapiens became an instant bother because he strongly believed that for one to pass in mathematics, caning was an integral ingredient. He would cane us then intone, "You will remember me one day and wish I had caned you harder." Well, I remember him. But he was wrong on the caning. As expected, we worked very hard to avoid caning, but instead of becoming overnight masters in the subject, we became more confused and terror-stricken.

On this day during prep, Henry Thige observed that our main handicap in the subject lay in a poor foundation.

"We have a negative attitude towards the subject and Mr. Sapiens Sapiens is not helping the situation," I intoned.

"I want to pass but I am afraid he will kill me before I do," Nero said.

We concurred that Mr. Sapiens Sapiens had our best interests at heart but his approach was counter-productive. Onsogo suggested that we share our sentiments with him. Nero suggested that we should send a representative. As expected, no one was willing to bell the cat. After a long deadlock, we agreed to face him as a class. This way we would share the responsibility of our move and the outcome. Evidently, the worst that could befall us was flogging. When I joined standard six, we had been seventeen. Inmates who did not fit academically were transferred to senior schools for a chance to undergo vocational training. Only five of us had remained. We decided to confront Mr. Sapiens Sapiens when he was in a jovial mood.

Eventually, the big moment came and Mr. Sapiens Sapiens listened to us with a smile dancing on his lips. As arranged, to depict the gravity of the issue at hand, each person had to say something. Thige, the most vocal among us, outlined our problem. "We are scared of you, which makes it hard to understand the subject," he finished.

"We really want to pass," I said.

"We believe we can pass," Onsogo concluded.

Having presented our case, we waited with bated breath for the worst.

"I only have one question," he said. "Are you teaching me how to teach you?"

"We just wanted to suggest…" I started.

"Get out before I lose my head."

His seemingly jovial mood had changed to that of a volcano threatening to erupt, and we left his tiny office in a hurry. For two weeks, he did not attend his lessons. When he eventually appeared in the third week, he declared that we would have a crash programme. Apart from the usual mathematics lesson hours, we would have an extra hour on weekdays from six in the evening. His teaching methodology changed as well. He would introduce the basics of a particular topic, give simple examples, then move to the standard eight syllabus. This took time and a lot of patience on his part.

The first sign of improvement became evident during the second term zonal exams. Not only did we record individual improvement in the subject, but we were number five in the zone. This caused a ripple of excitement and, confident that we had what it took, encouraged us to work harder. Divisional exams brought with them more improvement and excitement. Mr. Sapiens Sapiens continued to teach tirelessly and other teachers, challenged by his achievement, joined the race to improve their areas. By this time, the administration had so much faith in our ability to do well that we were relieved of all duties. At the dining hall, we were served first so that we could go back to class on time. By the time we sat for the mocks, we had become a force to reckon with.

On the eve of the exams, we attended a special mass in town with other candidates from the locality. I received a few success cards bearing all sorts of advice, encouragement and prayers. On the day of the exams, I felt I had prepared the best way possible, given the prevailing circumstances.

As I left for the December holidays, I was confident that I had done well in the exams. I waited impatiently for the results to see just how well. Finally, after Christmas, the results were released. There was jubilation and partying in the neighbourhood by those who had sat the same exam. Someone had scored 429 marks in the neighbourhood and become a celebrity overnight. For me to know my results, I had to travel all the way to school. That was an expensive undertaking which forced me to wait for the opening day in January.

I arrived in school to a heroic welcome. Alphonse Onsogo had scored 518, Wycliffe Nero 496, I had 495, Lawrence Mbwese 472 and Henry Thige 462. We were heroes. Somebody somewhere had decided that our class population was so small it would give undue competition to other schools if included in the national ranking. As a result, we missed our chance of appearing on television and newspapers, singing songs of jubilation. Everyone in the school was ecstatic, most notably Mr. Sapiens Sapiens who had triggered it all. After taking a photo together he said: "Sorry I cut you short on that day. What were you suggesting?"

"That you teach us the way you did," I said.

"I thought so."

"Now we are Homo Sapiens Sapiens too, aren't we?" Onsogo said amid roaring laughter.

"Well, consult Charles Darwin."

Our stint as champions was cut short by the arrival of admission letters. Academically speaking, we did not belong here. Standard eight was the farthest the school could take us. The administration was silent on our fate. Since we had no classes to attend, we became permanent faces in the kitchen so that by the end of January, each one of us had gained some weight.

To cut on the budget to the schools, the government had recently come up with an early release programme for those who had showed positive change and could be supported within the community. Henry Thige grabbed this opportunity and joined a public school. I still had two years to go and no one was willing to take care of me. The same happened to my three colleagues. As days went by, it became obvious that we would end up in a senior school to start vocational training. Now that it had come to that, I was at a loss deciding the best profession to take. I was torn between mechanics and carpentry.

I looked at the skies from the window of my hostel to view the thousands of stars decorating the still night. I had fought my battle to reach the farthest I could possibly go and hoped my mother was proud of me. She was one of the stars, shining bright, smiling down at me.

CHAPTER 15

I had grown used to being ordered into a vehicle and being taken to an undisclosed destination. As it were, I had resigned to my fate. This time around, only four of us occupied the rear of the school Land Rover as the accompanying staff and driver stayed in front. We enjoyed the country scene all the way to Nairobi, upon where we lost our sense of direction. The big city was like a gigantic jigsaw to us. Onsogo wondered what would happen if we were ordered out of the vehicle and left there.

"We would grow old trying to find our bearings," Nero retorted.

I had been in the city five years before and nothing seemed to have changed. The soot-stained street boys were still roaming the streets; the refuse heaps were still there. Human and motor traffic executed their helter-skelter dance heartily: fighting for space, honking, emitting gases to the already dense air; the boom-boom from their music systems only challenged by curses from drivers and shouts from touts as they fought to win commuters. Apparently, chaos was the accepted order. In their hurry, no one moved. It was bizarre that anyone got to where they were going.

After what seemed like an eternity, we realised we were getting out of town again.

"We are going to Getathuru," Mbwese observed.

"Wrong. Kabete," Nero said. Instead of entering the reception centre, we drove through an opposite gate. The sign post read: Kabete Approved School. We pulled up near the offices. Now that I was sure we had reached our destination, I stopped to survey my new home which could be regarded as the senior-most school because, while it admitted inmates from other schools, they were only released but never transferred. The buildings were old, white-washed and strewn about the vast compound. They could well be a century old, but still stood strong and bleak, a lasting proof that their builders had not been inspired by beauty but durability. The paths were lined up with flowers and white-washed stones. To the left, bordering the Artificial Insemination Centre, were the workshops – tailoring, welding, masonry, blacksmiths, mechanics and carpentry – huge, iron-sheet structures that spoke of age and neglect, their green paint peeling off, and an air of inactivity hanging obstinately upon them. Across the playing ground were new buildings coming up. Considering the battered look on the rest of the buildings, they looked out of place, like diamonds among stones. Whereas the old buildings had strong pillars, the new ones stood on steel structures with bricks skirting three quarters of the walls, with a louver completing it. They were seemingly removed from the rest of the compound, but the name on the main door screamed: Kabete Approved Secondary School. I felt like jumping with joy on reading the name. So I had not reached a dead end; there was a chance to continue with my studies. There, across the field was my lifeline.

Looking at the inmates hovering about the office, I knew I needed old friends at my side. They were huge and most had beards. But for their green uniforms, they could well pass for staff members. An important aspect of a subsequent transfer was the probability of a re-union with old friends who helped shield against bullying. But then, I could not spot a familiar face.

Everyone was full of praise for our performance. After the official reception, we were directed to the dormitory section. We were walking past the dining hall when I heard someone call my name. I turned to see the caller.

"Karanchu!" I exclaimed with relief. "How is the going?"

"Smooth like butter. I hear you performed very well," Karanchu said. "But then you were brainy. Personally I am in welding. I went to Dagoretti then was transferred here six months ago. It is a good place, really. I will show you around."

Two boys were sharing a cigarette behind one of the dormitories. This was a new experience to me. While I knew there were smokers at Othaya, no one ever did it in the open.

"These are my buddies. This is Ng'ash and that is Kelvin."

Kelvin passed the cigarette stick to Karanchu who puffed it as though his life depended on it. After a few puffs, he stretched his hand in my direction and I shook my head.

"Sorry I forget too fast. You are saved, right?"

I smiled. "I just don't smoke."

"Well, we love living dangerously."

Kelvin was a swarthy youth who didn't talk much. He had closely cropped hair and huge ear-lobes. When he talked, he praised Bob Marley and Haile Selassie. Kelvin was brown with shifty eyes. If sheng could be described as perfect, then his was.

A boy emerged from behind one of the dormitories, surveyed the area for a few moments, then disappeared.

"That is a dormitory captain, one of the holier-than-thou recruits who walk on foot across the road to join the secondary section. They are not like you and me. They simply don't belong. Just think about it. I have been around six years and he thinks he can order me around. Something tells him he joined Starehe Boys. I will send him packing."

A wildlife enthusiast had named the dormitories here. There was Kiboko, Simba, Nyati and Kifaru. I was in

Nyati. According to Karanchu, the dormitories were relics dating back to the First World War and were primarily meant to house horses. He supported his theory using the back wall of one of them which clearly showed there was once a huge opening that had been sealed off.

"Time to tour the neighbourhood," Karanchu declared picking a plastic bucket. He informed me matter-of-factly that there was no water in the school.

"We get it from a small stream some two kilometres away."

Every dormitory was allocated a full week to attend to kitchen matters: cook, clean utensils, fetch water and serve in the dining hall. To qualify for breakfast, one had to fetch a bucket full of water and split ten pieces of firewood. The same applied to supper. Thus, while on duty, the first thing in the morning and after classes was to pick a bucket and go in search of water. Someone had come up with a bright idea of sinking a borehole, but the project was still underway.

Supper was served at six and we lined up in front of the dining hall. The dining captain gave a long speech about failure to fetch water and warned against going for a second helping. He reported that during lunch time, ten inmates had missed food because of this vice. He was tough and spoke with a lot of authority.

I was enjoying my bowl of beans, a piece of meat and ugali when this inmate stretched his hand to pick my piece of meat. I moved my bowl and raised my head to face him. Our eyes locked for a long moment. He was big and heavily built. He had a set of two huge eyes that gave him an open face. I didn't know what kind of devil he was but I decided I did not care. He might have been older than me in the school but that gave him no right to terrorise me. I picked the piece of meat and started munching it. Meanwhile, he got on his feet and leaned across the table.

"You will be sorry for this," he whispered in my ear.

Just then, a huge man in a box hairstyle stepped on the dais and switched off the television set. All eyes turned in his direction.

"Today we are privileged to have visitors," he said in perfect English. "I believe they are joining the secondary section. Gentlemen, let me take this opportune moment to congratulate and welcome you to the only national school in the republic where you don't pay a cent and there are no cut-off marks."

There was laughter and clapping. I didn't need to be told that he was the school captain. Why, he was born for the task. Unlike the dining captain who sounded abrasive, the man in front sounded friendly yet very firm. Even the staff members about hung on every word he uttered. His hand gestured, hammering his points home. I immediately wanted to know his story. What did he do to become an inmate? Where did he learn to speak English so well? I came to learn that his name was Alexander Mwenda but inmates called him Malcolm X or simply X.

I accompanied Karanchu outside the dining hall. "Who is he?" I said pointing at the inmate I had just collided with.

"KB. Kazi Bure. He lives to eat and look after cattle. The joke is that he is long overdue for release but the administration fears he will commit suicide if he is sent off."

I was allocated the same dormitory with KB and Karanchu. My bed was above that of Junge, the taekwondo captain who religiously lifted weights made of two bricks connected with a metal bar every morning and evening. He was heavily muscled and loved to display it. Like tough men in movies, he rarely put on a shirt. He was the kind everyone wanted to befriend.

After bringing each other up to speed with Karanchu till ten in the night, I retired. I was dead beat hence immediately I covered myself, I fell asleep. Then my mind travelled into the future in a dream. I had completed school and was working in a skyscraper somewhere in the city. It had been a long day and I took the lift to the basement where my car was waiting at the parking lot. There was no traffic on the city roads and within no time I was home. My wife ran to welcome me. Nostalgia seized me as I recalled meeting and falling for Anastasia on our first day in nursery school. On the table were various delicacies that whetted my appetite. I was so hungry that I forgot to wash my hands and grabbed a chicken leg. My wife was busy warning me that I should wash my hands when I felt something cold run against my thigh. I kicked my blanket off only to see a silhouette running away. There was movement in the bed below and a while later, someone switched on the lights. I found myself facing a very irate Junge.

"How dare you urinate on me?"

"It is water," I said in a desperate attempt to escape his wrath. "Someone poured it on me. Just smell it." Karanchu was a heavy sleeper. I repeated what I had just said louder in an attempt to wake him up but he was probably dead. Junge looked at me for a long moment as if deciding on the best way to kill me. To my utter relief, he reached for the blanket and smelt it. He looked hard at me then his eyes travelled round the room. Half the dormitory was now awake. Junge's eyes rested on KB. While other inmates appeared sleepy KB was very much awake. Junge walked towards him at a painfully slow pace. Sensing danger, KB sprung to a sitting position. Junge seized him by the collar and yanked him out of bed.

"What is so wonderful about sleeping on a wet bed?"

"What do you mean?" KB asked apprehensively.

"His admission number is 9186," Junge said pointing a thick finger at me. "Everyone is singing how well he passed his KCPE. That is not someone who can wet his bed. Besides, that is water. I witnessed your little brawl at the dining hall. Is this your way of settling it?"

"I don't know what you are talking about."

Junge released him and took a bucketful of water and was about to pour it on KB's bed.

"Okay, okay! It is me. I am sorry."

"Apologise to him."

KB walked to me awkwardly and apologised.

"To prove that you are really sorry you will exchange bedding for the night."

# CHAPTER 16

If we had everything we wanted, then we would cherish nothing at all. We buy new garments, brag about them, boast about how special they are then, within no time, discard them because they are out of fashion. Lovers stand up against the world to live together, exchange vows to be one till death put them asunder, then live fighting, even killing one another to live alone. Discontent and more discontent - the tragedy of life. Things that are out of reach, like a trip to heaven, remain forever attractive. A wise man noticed this and quipped that grass is always greener on the other side.

Initially, being in secondary school seemed like an adventure. This changed quickly to become a challenge and, to some extent, a bother. I found myself counting my problems, real and imagined, instead of working hard at my studies. Back in primary school, answers were on test papers and one just had to choose whether the correct one was A, B, C, or D. The correct answer could be as awkward as 'none of the above' or 'all of the above'. In secondary school, one had to carry the answers into the examination room – in the head, that is. New and challenging subjects like chemistry and physics were introduced. Again, it was a new school with serious challenges due to lack of teachers and learning materials.

We were twenty-two by the end of first term, most inmates having joined from public schools. They were irritatingly full of themselves and self-righteous and I fully concurred with Karanchu that they did not belong. They didn't blend in; they were like recruits amongst soldiers in a battlefield. Over the years, inmates had cultivated the culture of standing by one another, but the new kids on the block did not only rejoice in ratting, they fought to beat one another at it. They created the impression of being lesser inmates. The most notorious was Jackson Matendechero, evidently one of the brightest inmates but incurably egocentric. After coming tops in first term, he was behaving like a demigod.

By the time we were in form two, the class population had increased to thirty-five. One morning, ten of the newcomers were sent packing. Apparently, someone somewhere had discovered a gold mine. He told interested parents there was a free secondary school and all one had to do was cough up two thousand shillings for admission.

Evidently, the institution needed to fine-tune its approach to discipline and correction because disappearance of items was a normal occurrence: bowls from the kitchen, maize from the fields and blankets from the dormitories. On and off, someone milked the cows at night. On one occasion, someone escaped with all the beef from the kitchen.

By and by, I found the need for money pressing. To survive, I would do menial jobs such as tilling and fetching water for the staff members. While in form three, the matron contracted me to be fetching water for her on a monthly basis. I would get Kshs. 250 for my sweat. She had two very beautiful daughters, Kate and Juliet. Kate's brown skin, sensual mouth, flowing hair and sleepy eyes reminded me of Anastasia. The two were so proud they hardly talked to me. You can therefore understand my astonishment when on this morning, I found Karanchu admiring the picture of a girl.

"That is Kate!" I said. Karanchu turned to look at me, wearing a winning grin. "How did you get that?"

"Simple. I just told her I needed it."

I studied him for a long moment. "I mean, how do they take it because of where you attend school?"

He looked at me incredulously. "What has it got to do with anything? Are you afraid of girls?"

"No, not particularly," I said. "There is this girl in my neighbourhood. She is the most beautiful thing I have ever seen. When she smiles, she reminds me of the morning sun. When I look at her, I go weak in the knees. Trouble is, I can't put my feelings into words simply because I dread a rejection."

"You have never approached her," he observed. "Why conclude that she will reject you?"

"Back there, no one trusts me." Karanchu chuckled.

"That's the trouble with residing in the countryside. Folks there love meddling in other people's affairs. In town, everyone is too engrossed in making ends meet to care. Heavens, girls fight over me!"

He looked at me like a mother looking at her hungry baby. "It is no big deal, really. I have a solution for you. See me in the evening when we go to fetch water."

My admiration for Karanchu's resourcefulness was growing by the minute. No problem was too big or complex for him to handle. I could hardly wait to learn from the master. Anyone who could acquire a photo from Kate was worth admiration and imitation. I imagined his kind of solution and several possibilities crossed my mind. He could fix a date and take me through the paces. For girls to fight over him, he probably had a love potion. Well, I only had to wait.

I felt that the burden of winning Anastasia over was off my shoulders, hence I got lost in imagining life with her. I imagined walking with her in the woods, holding hands. The thought made all my problems ebb away. She seemed like a well of joy whose company was a solution to sorrow, hunger and even death. My attraction to her was like an all-consuming fire with heavenly promise. She had become an obsession. My mind would drift to her even when the teacher was in class. I would spend a lot of time writing romantic lines I planned to use to win her over. While at home, I would lie in wait for her at the local shopping centre in the evening, but immediately she appeared, my mind would go blank. I had a fatal attraction towards her, coupled with a profound dread of rejection.

On this day, the geography teacher was busy explaining features produced by wind in the desert when I recalled a romantic line and decided to write it down.

I miss you like the desert misses the rain.

I imagined Anastasia reading it and my mind raced. I lifted my eyes to see the teacher staring at me.

"We don't have all day," he said. Everyone was looking at me and it dawned on me that I had been daydreaming for several minutes. The teacher walked to my desk and picked my book up.

"Step in front and read it aloud."

I went to the front of the class sweating all over. I had been caught pants down and I was about to be embarrassed in front of the class.

"Roses are more beautiful than lilies, but you are more beautiful than them all," I started. "There is only one girl who is more beautiful than you; look in the mirror and you will see her. I miss you like the desert misses the rain."

The class started laughing as the teacher studied me sternly and ordered me to repeat what I had just read ten times.

"What is her name?" It reminded me of my class teacher at Kiambiriria Primary School asking my name.

"Anastasia."

"Let this be the first and last warning."

Immediately the four o'clock bell rang, I ran to the dormitory, picked my bucket and went to look for Karanchu. As expected, he was in the company of Kelvin and Ng'ash who was busy narrating about a new matatu with the loudest music and most artistic decorations. He swore to board it in his next journey to town, even if it meant waiting for it the whole day. He had a fresh Ray Parker haircut.

We started our journey. To get to the water point, we followed a winding track through a thicket. The track had diversions which I had never used. Karanchu left the main track and took a diversion to the left.

"Where to?"

"Base," he said. "Relax, will you?"

I did my best to relax and trailed them. I had no idea what 'base' meant and I was eager to learn. The path was a cul-de-sac, with a clearing of about seven square feet canopied by the thicket. There was a log which acted as a bench.

"Is this the base?" Karanchu nodded.

"Do you want to fight shyness and be as confident as a lion? Do you want to forget poverty and embrace abundance? Do you want to fly? Do you want emancipation?"

"I do," I said, nodding vigorously.

"That is easy."

From his breast pocket he removed a cigarette stick – no, a stick like a cigarette, because it was thicker than the normal cigarette. It lacked the fine finish of a manufacturing factory. This, coupled with the fact that it lacked a filter, made it look crude. It reminded me of an old man back home who smoked dried tobacco leaves rolled onto an old newspaper. Then it came to me in a flash.

Marijuana!

"Is this…"

"This is it. Just take a puff."

I had heard of marijuana and strange stories: of eating insatiably, of working tirelessly, of fighting, of running mad, of going bananas, and of becoming a zombie. Some said it took ten solid years for a puff to get out of the body. Those were stories. Karanchu was standing in front of me assuring me that it would give me wings. It would also make me forget that I was an inmate who was not readily welcome in the society, let alone a girl's heart. The three were waiting for me patiently. It was my big day; thus I would get the first puff. I thought of Anastasia and all the terrifying stories ebbed away. I took the thick stick and stuck it in my mouth. Karanchu lit it for me. I did not take one puff, I took three. I was so determined and was about to take the fourth one when Karanchu took the stick and he and his friends started sharing it.

Then I grew wings – well, if the experience I was going through was what Karanchu had meant. My mind felt very light. I was swimming in the air. My colleagues appeared funny and I roared with laughter. Then I looked at myself and discovered that my hands were missing. I could not imagine life without hands and I started wailing. I had to report the loss as fast as possible. The path out of 'base' had disappeared and was replaced by a wide road. It seemed the only way out and I followed it. Someone seized me by the collar and swung me around. I felt like Goliath and that was all the vexation I needed to beat him up. I threw a side kick only to be knocked on my head, and I blacked out.

The next day, I woke up to mock laughter. When I studied those who were laughing, I discovered that it was directed at me. Ng'ash was the man of the moment. He stretched his arms and talked in a sorrowful voice. "Look, teacher, look! They cut my hands." He could not go on and he roared with laughter.

"We had to buy him some milk to bring him back to earth."

"How many puffs did he take?" someone wanted to know.

"Just one," Ng'ash said amid shrill laughter. I found myself laughing too.

Three weeks later, Karanchu was released. We sat outside the gate as he waited for a bus to town.

"I will miss you," I said. "Remember that escape at Kericho? You were amazing! What plans do you have?"

"Just one: to get rich."

We were silent for a long moment.

"How come you started cutting grass for Mrs. Kange'the?" I asked. "You are not the type."

"That is a clever observation," he said conspiratorially. "There was this girl who wanted a new dress and I was hard up. We were given new blankets and my mind went to work."

"Heavens above!" I quipped as I added two and two. I recalled the day we found all the blankets gone. "You established yourself as the man on the job and, after fooling everyone, you stuffed the blankets in the sacks, topped them up with grass then transported them!"

"In fact I was assisted to carry them to the road to catch my bus. I must be going. So long!"

My mouth hung open in awe as Karanchu boarded the bus.

I was in form three, in my second term, when changes that completely altered the face of the school occurred. We were given new uniforms; grey trousers and a sweater, a light blue shirt and a navy blue tie. We were smart and confident. You should have seen us admiring ourselves.

The new dormitories were completed. Rumours started going round that soon we would be relocating. The day dawned and we received official communication. We were ecstatic. We dashed across the playing field with our belongings.

My prayers for being baptized were answered. I had always admired Daniel's courage when he was thrown into the lion's den, hence I was baptized Daniel Muthini. I could not drop my mother's name just yet because officially I was Muthini Njoki.

Then a new manager, Mr. Joseph Kenyenya, arrived. He was a steadfast, no-nonsense man and his inaugural speech said it all.

"My employer told me I was joining a correctional facility, but your actions tell me that this is a place where one can do anything he likes, taking his sweet time at it. It gives me the impression that to some of you, this is a fattening camp, while to most of you, the greatest and only achievement is witnessing the day break and dusk set in. I have news for you: that ends this very moment. You should get an education, and vocational training. Consequently, you need a very good reason – I doubt there is one–to be out of class or workshop. The government pays these teachers because of you; make use of them. After seven, everyone, including the captain, should be in class for preps. Lateness will be punished. Your days for taking a stroll in the park are over!"

It was a new dawn.

# CHAPTER 17

For the first time, I was not interested in the scenery outside the windows of the home-bound bus. Not that I could see much because, as usual, I was standing at the aisle sandwiched between taller passengers. My mind was busy calculating my impending encounter with Anastasia. Karanchu's strategy was out. Win or lose, I did not require his kind of wings. I simply had to believe in myself. If girls fell for romantic lines, I had several. If they went for physical features, I was more handsome than a lot of married men. As far as school was concerned, well, girls fought over Karanchu.

Immediately I disembarked from the bus, I went straight home and changed. I then went to the village to trace Anastasia. I saw her, but she was in the company of her mother. I got an opportunity three days later.

"How is school?" I ventured after exchanging greetings.

"Okay."

I was tense and I cursed the fact. My romantic lines had evaporated. We walked a few paces then I said: "There is something I want to tell you."

"Save your breath. You love me."

I nodded vigorously and relaxed. This was going to be easy, after all.

"I knew that from our days in school."

"To say that I love you is putting it mildly. I just can't live without you."

"Really?"

"Look," I had been energised. "Whoever said that the beautiful ones are not yet born had not seen you."

"I never knew you were so romantic."

"I may not be. Just looking at you inspires me."

She smiled coyly. "I want to know one thing."

"Anything, anytime. Just ask."

"Why did they take you to Wamumu?"

The question sapped energy out of me and I started sweating all over.

"My mother could not pay for my education and..."

"If you love me then open your heart. What did you steal?"

Her voice was full of malice. She was taunting me and enjoying it. If people started off on such a sour note and sublimed into husband and wife, then they possessed qualities I was not bestowed with. Despite a concerted effort to keep my anger under control, I was losing it.

"Okay," I said, fighting to keep my voice down. "What is in your mind?"

"You are not the only one who dropped out because of money."

"True."

"So, what did you steal? If I have to love a thief, I need to know what they stole and how they did it. I swear I will never tell anyone."

Sometimes I am rather hot–tempered. This was such an instance. I was so mad I almost hit her. Something told me that pursuing the conversation would make me do something I would later regret. I turned and hit the road walking as fast as I could. I thought I heard her giggle.

Why was everyone behaving so strangely? Why the negative attitude; why the mistrust; why…? Would it ever end? Heavens above, I was innocent! I desperately wanted to prove the fact. But how? I needed to be seen for what I was, to be appreciated for my true worth.

After deep thought, I was more galled with myself than with Anastasia. Why, she had only confirmed my fears and my reaction was deplorable. Despite knowing that I was innocent, I was more bothered by what other people thought of me. I lived with the fear of their wrong conclusions to the extent of taking marijuana so that I could portray a different character. I came to the bitter conclusion that I could not change a thing. The fact was I could not rewrite history. That I was arrested, gone through a remand home, Getathuru, Kericho, Othaya and now Kabete was indelible, unalterable and a fabric of my very existence. No matter how zealous I was to change and impress them, I remained Daniel Muthini Njoki;

an innocent inmate – a very blessed person given the circumstances. Convincing the masses of my innocence was impossible.

I recalled a line I had seen somewhere and wrote it down: If it is not necessary to do it, it is necessary not to do it. I read it again and again. I read it aloud. It had all the wisdom I ever needed. Why, I didn't need to prove anything to anyone. I owed no one an apology: not Anastasia, not my relatives, not the society. After being kicked out of school, I had spent two years of hopelessness and no one came to my rescue. Now that I was back in class, they didn't approve of my school. But no one offered an alternative. Apparently, the only acceptable option to them would have been staying out of school. I only needed to quench my thirst for education. Oh yes, that was necessary.

This conclusion gave me new energy. I felt as if I had passed the form four exams already. I was unstoppable. I had done it once in standard eight; I was in form three and could do it again. This time it was tougher and there were more challenges, but I would not give up. To succeed, I needed a realistic plan. I needed proper time management. I retrieved my report forms and studied them carefully.

I fared well in the arts but was poor in the sciences. Whereas I could get eighty percent in geography, I scored as little as thirty percent in chemistry. Thus, even if I dedicated all my time to geography and, by any chance scored a hundred per cent, I could only add twenty marks. I would then lose seventy marks in chemistry, or more. The trick was in giving each and every subject equal attention and a little bit more to the ones I was poorest in. I was taking seven subjects and I decided to allocate a subject to each day of the week. Mathematics was the toughest and I would practise it everyday.

I would no longer fetch water. I needed some coins to get by, but then I needed the time more.

Charting my way forward was the easy part. I would be lying if I said I had no feelings for Anastasia. I still did and knew they would not just ebb away. I required a concerted effort to overcome them. But I resolved to keep her – or any other girl for that matter – at bay. This was not the time; their time would come.

On this day, I was walking from the coffee factory when this girl, a former classmate at Kiambirira Primary School, caught up with me. She had walked really fast to catch up with me but upon reaching me, she reduced her speed to fall into step with me.

"Good heavens!" she exclaimed, "this sun will bake us alive."

"Well," I said. "We have survived it before. We only forget too fast."

She smiled revealing a set of milk-white teeth. She had grown into a beauty to behold.

"The name is Agnes…."

"Wangechi."

"You surely have a superb memory," she said. "How is school?"

"Fine."

"I mean, do they teach you well…?"

I didn't hear the rest of what she said because I lost my temper. I lost my temper because she brought back memories of Anastasia asking me what I had stolen. I lost my temper because she had the confidence to pry into my life.

"Next you will be asking what I stole and if they cane me for breakfast, lunch and supper."

"What?"

I stopped and faced her. "Exactly what do you want?"

"Look, I mean…," She had lost her confidence. She was worried. The hunter had become the hunted. She started walking and I followed her. We negotiated the corner and came upon her mother and a neighbour. They were talking excitedly, but when they saw us, they stopped in their tracks.

Agnes quickened her pace.

# CHAPTER 18

This was a four-week holiday but I found it too long. I had planned to have a memorable time but as it were, it had not worked. Now I had my plan to excel in academics and I was dying to kick-start it. Funny, I thought, that I should miss school. Going back to school was a welcome but short-term relief. I only had a year to go after which I would have to live among these people.

"You are disturbed," my cousin Patrick observed.

"Well, we have the exact thing to lift up your spirits."

Jeff, one of his school mates, had visited. He was from a rich family and his clothing was a fashion statement of the day. His Chicago Bulls cap was tilted to the side; his shoes, jeans and T-shirt were a size too big. Looking at him, I knew where my cousin got his inspiration. Keeping pace with Jeff put a serious strain on his father financially. He ought to have cleared form four but he had been expelled from his former school and joined his present school one class behind.

Looking at Jeff, I knew we could not fit in one basket. He was pompous; and why not, he was from a rich family. Whereas I never had a birthday party in my life, his father bought him a car on his seventeenth birthday. Driven chiefly by jealousy, I decided to spoil myself by sharing in his bliss.

We picked Patrick's girlfriend at the gate of her homestead. Nelly was short, chocolate-complexioned and about seventeen years. Her head was bald and she wore the biggest earrings I had ever seen. Her blouse did not cover her back. To crown it all, she donned a miniskirt and high heels.

We proceeded to the shopping centre and stopped.

"Where is she?" Jeff asked, scanning the area.

"There."

You could have knocked me with a feather as I saw the girl walking towards the car. Anastasia! She looked glamorous in a floral dress. Her hair was done in delicate zig zag lines. Then I noticed it; her necklace, earrings, belt, bangles and open shoes were all pink. Her eyebrows were pink too!

She didn't care to greet the rest of us as she occupied the front seat.

I immediately got forgotten. I liked it that way.

We were on a rough road doing a hundred kilometres an hour. Apparently, I was the only one who could notice the speed because Jeff had one hand on the steering wheel and the other on Anastasia, whose head rested on his chest. Patrick and Nelly were lost to the world next to me. Something told me I should not be in the car but the thought of trekking back home kept me in check. We went round a corner and I saw an old man on a bicycle. "Watch out!" I shouted. Jeff swerved to the left missing the ditch narrowly.

"Holy cow!" Patrick said.

"What is wrong with this country?" Jeff shouted over the blast from the stereo. "For heavens sake this is a vehicle and he ought to give way!"

"He had the right of way," I observed. Jeff brought the car to a screeching halt, switched off the stereo and turned to face me. "Who is this clown?"

"He is my cousin," Patrick said.

Anastasia turned and our eyes locked for a very long moment. Jeff was shaking with rage. "I don't like people reprimanding me. Even in school, teachers know better."

Tension was high as we resumed our journey. We stopped at a small shopping centre where Jeff and Anastasia entered into a bar. They emerged fifteen minutes later with Jeff smoking a cigarette.

"I can't wait for the boat ride," Patrick said. Jeff puffed hard at his cigarette and handed it to me. I shook my head and he looked at me quizzically. "Oh, I get it. You are used to heavier stuff. Marijuana. Heroin, maybe?"

I quickly turned my attention to Anastasia. She must have briefed Jeff about where I went to school.

We resumed our journey. After three kilometres, we came upon a dam and stopped. A ragged-looking man sat on a home-made boat at the shore. His face lifted in anticipation and, as if to declare he was ready for us, stood up and stretched. He wore a torn overall and a hat whose brim was almost falling off.

After some haggling, it was agreed that a trip round the dam would cost us two hundred shillings. After boarding the boat the man pushed it into the water and then joined us. Twenty minutes later, we were at the middle of the dam, some hundred and fifty metres to dry land on all sides. The man whistled continuously as though the act gave him some strength. His hands were busy on the oar propelling us forward. Maybe the lake was not very popular or people were engaged elsewhere on this day.

"Wow!" Patrick exclaimed. "This is heaven."

Nelly started a song and the others joined in.

"Where is the source of this water?" I ventured.

"Underground," the man said.

"What is the name of the dam," I asked.

"We call it Karia Dam," he replied.

"Are there animals living here?"

"Yes," the man said keeping rhythm with his hands on the oars. "Small fish and hippos."

Conversation ceased in mid-sentences as all eyes turned to look at the man. His jaw was set, his eyes fixed at a point far ahead. To my utter consternation, he resumed whistling. My eyes scanned the water expanse expecting to see a yawning hippo. I even imagined it crushing me and cursed having boarded the home-made boat.

"You didn't tell us this," Anastasia said.

"You didn't ask," he said. "I need my dues. Now."

"We will pay when we are safely back on dry land," Jeff said.

"Last time you said the same."

The two men faced each other. "I never forget a face, particularly of a swindler. Last time you refused to pay me, remember? You had a different girl."

Jeff's face clouded and it was clear he remembered. He avoided Anastasia's questioning look.

"I want all my dues now," the man said emphatically. His eyes had narrowed to slits. Looking at him, one could safely conclude that he was down to his last option. Jeff chuckled, startling all of us.

"Do you know who I am?"

"You are just like my little boy at home waiting for something to eat. Have you ever been hungry?"

"My father is the police boss…."

"Really? Well, you are lucky. My money please," the man said stretching his hand. "I will count up to three. If you don't…,"

"Are you threatening me?"

Suddenly everyone wanted to talk at once. In the process of shouting each other down, the boat lost balance and we swerved dangerously.

"We can solve this…," I started.

"Shut up!" Jeff commanded.

"No. You shut up!" It was Anastasia. "Who was that girl you were with?"

Just then the man dived into the water taking the oar with him. The boat almost capsized, scooping some water. The girls started crying.

"Do you want to kill us?" Jeff asked.

"I cannot swim!" Anastasia wailed. I recalled my swimming stint at Othaya and was afraid the expertise gained was hardly adequate for the task at hand.

"I don't want to die," Nelly sobbed.

"Sometimes it doesn't pay to be abrasive," Patrick addressed Jeff. "We are at his mercy."

The man floated in the water as though he were dead. He had caught us flat-footed and knew it.

"If he hurts me in any way my father…" the man started swimming away and the girls wailed in unison. "Okay, okay, okay!" Jeff shouted. He fished out a bundle of notes, prompting the man to rejoin us in the boat. Jeff gave him four hundred shillings.

"Thanks," the man said. "Thanks a lot."

The still water had lost its allure and no one was interested in continuing with the tour. No one spoke on the return journey, which seemed to take longer than expected.

"By the way," the man said once we were on dry land. "There are no hippos. Feel most welcome."

I arrived home at seven, only to find a plastic paper bag at the doorway to the house. Since it was at my doorstep, I assumed it was meant for me. I took it, entered the house, lit the lamp then opened it. Inside were seven revision books: form three and four mathematics, physics and chemistry, commerce and two revision books for geography and history. God had clearly heard my prayers and sent a Good Samaritan. I promptly started working on them.

I had been working for four solid hours when the lamp ran out of kerosene. Something was troubling me. Who had brought the books? The fact that they were outside the door meant that whoever brought them had not found someone to leave them with because my grandmother always went to bed at six.

"Who brought the books?" I asked her at breakfast.

"What books?"

That said it all. She wasn't aware of the existence of the books. I was going through geography when a note fell from the pages. It read thus:

I am sorry I offended you on that day. I need not pry into your life; I know all about your school because my cousin was there. If the arm of the law was long enough, half of the youth would be there. It is not the uniform you wear that says what you are; it is the things you do.

I hope these books will be useful.

Agnes

I read the note again and again. My heart was full of remorse, my legs felt weak and I had to sit down. It was disturbing to realise that while others were busy condemning me, I was condemning people of goodwill as well. I was like a man possessed as I started towards the gate. I ran all the way to Agnes' homestead. Her younger brother was just leaving.

"Is Agnes home?"

"No," he said and studied me keenly. "Are you her boyfriend?"

"No. Where is she?"

"Nairobi," he answered curtly and hurried on.

School would be opening the following day, so I returned home to prepare myself.

# CHAPTER 19

There is a saying that people appreciate their cow's ability to produce a lot of milk only after it dies. A few weeks into first term, the manager, Mr. Kenyenya, the man who had established himself and greatly succeeded as a reformer, was transferred and replaced by a lady, Miss Wambua. Whereas Mr. Kenyenya was experienced, authoritative, firm and sometimes autocratic, his successor was a soft novice. Things started running out of hand overnight as apathy set in among staff members. Mr. Kenyenya had valued the well-being and academic development of the inmates and had been tough on his staff in order to attain his objectives. His departure was seen as a win for the staff and a loss by the inmates. Some of the inmates close to the manager said that the staff had ganged up against him and forced him out somehow.

Then, in a surprise move, the new manager kicked out Malcolm X as the captain. This aggravated the already worsening backlash against Mr. Kenyenya's transfer. Mwenda had a nose for opportunity and he quickly started rallying the inmates against the administration. Much as there was more than enough to complain about,

X wanted to settle scores. A day was set for presenting our grievances to the Director of Children's Services. The message was only whispered with a stern warning that letting the cat out of the bag would attract dire consequences. In a show of solidarity, the whole form four class would go. I recalled facing Mr. Sapiens Sapiens at Othaya and smiled at the inherent tendency of history to repeat itself. Whereas the Othaya incident was remedial, the current one was confrontational. As X put it, it was better to die on one's feet than to live on one's knees.

On the D-day, we hit the road at five. We flagged down a Kenya Bus which was on its way to town. No one had money and if anyone did, no one would dare pay. The plan was simple. We would line up along the aisle. The ones in front would say someone at the back would pay. The ones at the rear would say someone in front would pay. Most probably the bus would be packed and by the time the conductor realised that no one was paying, we would have covered several kilometres.

"You have grown cold feet," Matendechero said as our bus sped towards the city. He was a close friend of the transferred manager and had taken it personally. "You are not comfortable with this," he said emphatically. "You never were from the very beginning."

"Look, I am in this bus standing next to you. What makes you a hero?"

He placed his left ear on my stomach. "His stomach is swarming with butterflies," he said and chuckled. Inmates next to us were now absorbed in his little act. "But then what would anyone expect? He loves sitting on the fence. He never had a strong backbone." My rage was starting to boil. He was bigger and more energetic, but I could no longer withstand him.

There was commotion at the front of the bus. The conductor was shouting and the bus came to a screeching halt. We were flushed out. After five minutes, another bus appeared and we flagged it down. We were kicked out of three buses before we decided to walk the rest of the journey because by this time, we were near the office.

A surprise was waiting for us at the director's office. Miss Wambua, her arms akimbo, was standing outside the entrance to the building. Somehow, she had learnt of our mission.

"Hello boys," she said. "Have you lost your way to the classroom?"

Malcolm X was leading the way and he ignored her completely. We did likewise. She had no option but to trail us. The director arrived a few minutes to eight and suggested we elect two representatives. The two were in the office for half an hour. The director addressed us saying that he had noted our concerns and would be acting on them. The school vehicle came to pick us up.

The following day, the minister for Home Affairs and National Heritage, Honourable Polisi Lotodo, arrived at 6.30 a.m. in a convoy. He immediately went to the kitchen and asked for a bowl of porridge. He took a sip in full view of eager inmates. An ever stern-faced man, it was hard to deduce whether the porridge made him happy or infuriated him and we hoped it infuriated him and that someone was in real hot soup. He boarded his vehicle and left without talking to anyone. A week ended within which the school seemed to have changed completely. Teachers were on their toes, the food was superb and the inmates felt on top of the world. Malcolm X was a hero.

Then the director paid us a visit one morning and everything changed again. He was in the company of five men who looked senior and ten police officers. All staff members and inmates were ordered to the parade ground.

"You obviously don't appreciate it but you are very lucky because there are thousands of youths who would want to be in your place," the director started. "The government has invested a lot of resources in you so that you can fit in the society and earn a decent livelihood. But then what do you give in return? You want to dictate to the said government. You want to dictate who works where, when and with whom." He stopped to chuckle. He continued to pace as though he was inspecting a guard of honour. "Most of those in the secondary section are above eighteen, long past their release date. However, while we close our eyes so that you can benefit, your behaviour has proved that you don't need an education but reformation. Well, for that, you are beyond us now. You belong to Kamiti Maximum Prison."

He stopped near me and looked at me long and hard. He continued with his speech, still looking at me. "We were at pains to explain your presence after the expiry of the court stipulation. What if you burn down the institution? Now that you are so energetic after being fed dutifully, what if you beat up Miss. Wambua here? Those are tough questions." He continued to pace.

"For the misguided few, this is not an institution where you convene overnight meetings then wake up shouting, 'Our rights!' Some of you did that elsewhere and that is why you ended up here, to be reformed."

He walked to the front. "Since some of you cannot justify their stay here, we will see you off. We have done our best to mould you, to prepare you so that you blend with the society in a lawful manner. Nevertheless, it seems some of you were born outlaws. Well, it is time prisons took over. If I call your name, accompany these police officers and clear with us. Once you are through, you will be escorted out of the compound. Don't come back. I repeat, for your own sake do not ever come back."

Tension was sky-high now among the inmates. No one had anticipated this turn of events. That most of us in the secondary section were long overdue for release was very true. Gone were the days when we would dash for freedom; there was a lot to be gained in staying put. Being kicked out was a serious setback. It meant the end of formal education because no school would touch a drop-out inmate. The mere thought of studying all the way to form four only to hit a dead end was traumatic enough. Whereas Malcolm X was an obvious culprit, the rest of us could only pray that we were not on the list. We didn't know the number of the victims or how the administration had come up with the names.

I closed my eyes as I tried to recall how it all started. The arrest, the police station, remand home, Getathuru… an expulsion would be a big loss.

"Alexander Mwenda!" the director shouted. It was hard to deduce what was going on inside X's head as he walked casually to the front. For someone being expelled, he was too collected. But then, there were ten police officers dying for some action. While he possessed impressive leadership traits, Mwenda could only be described as an average student.

"Andrew Odeny."

"You called me?" Odeny said in shock. He stood near me. "I have done nothing. I …," he did not finish because two policemen seized him. He always took pride in being a confidant of the transferred manager.

"Is anyone willing to join the two?" the director asked. "None. You can stay and benefit or you can be expelled. The choice is yours."

He started towards his car with his entourage on his heels. His departure set in a new order. Inmates lost their voices, leaving the staff walking tall. The mood in the school was uncomfortably restrained. Emotions were still high but the price to pay was costly. To avoid victimisation people talked in whispers.

The last person one could expect to temper the mood was Kelvin. He was a confessed Rastafarian. Under the lid of his locker, was a huge portrait of Bob Marley and Haile Selassie. He rarely talked, something we believed was the consequence of smoking marijuana.

Usually after breakfast, we all trooped to the chapel for morning prayers. On this Wednesday, Kelvin was the first to arrive in the chapel armed with a Bible. To make sure that he was the one to lead the prayers, he stood at the pulpit. He waited patiently, his face sombre as usual, with only his eyes acknowledging our arrival. He was the last person we expected at the pulpit and a general murmur filled the chapel. Then he raised his hand for silence.

"This is the word for the day," Kelvin started. You could have heard a pin drop. "O, prince's daughter! The joints of thy thighs are like jewels, the work of the hands of a cunning workman. Thy navel is like a round goblet, which wanteth not liquor: thy belly is like a heap of wheat set about with lilies. Thy two breasts are like two young roes that are twins," Kelvin closed the book. "That is the word of the Lord."

There was uncontrollable laughter now but his face remained sombre as he stepped from the pulpit. Something was seriously troubling my mind: did he make it up or was it really in the Bible? I wanted someone to clarify and I turned to see the chaplain standing next to me. Shock was written all over his face.

# CHAPTER 20

As I went about my activities, the director's last words echoed in my mind. ' You can stay and benefit or you can be expelled. The choice is yours.' I wanted to benefit. My mother had urged me to fight like a wounded lion and this was my battlefield. I therefore did the best I could to tow the line.

You can therefore understand my confusion when I was summoned to the manager's office. I sat watching her arrange her table. She wanted to make me nervous and she succeeded. I cleared my throat to remind her of my presence.

"How is the going?" she asked oddly. Her question sent my mind into high gear. The going was tough, of course, but confessing such was like walking on a field of land mines. She was prying and I felt uncomfortable.

"Smooth."

She smiled benignly and stood up. "You must be wondering why I called you. I thought it prudent to hear from the students to get the true picture of this place. Maybe I have relied so much on my staff to run this institution. I know it is hard to trust me. Well, there is very little I can do to change that. That aside, I don't intend to spy. I am more interested in moving forward in harmony than victimising anyone. I chose you because you seem to have a sense of purpose. You seem focused."

She occupied her chair. "So how can we improve the situation?"

She was young and fresh from campus. She was worried that things were running out of hand.

"This is the only school I know and don't know how other schools run," I said.

"You need not. This is a unique institution which cannot run on the ethos of public schools. We need to think within the context of a correction centre."

"I cannot speak for the others. Personally, I just want an academic environment."

"Exactly how can we achieve that?"

"More books and teachers."

She was thoughtful for a long while. I had only stated the obvious and the only reason she could be thoughtful was because the meeting was not working according to her plan.

"Are the staff members okay?" The question brought memories of Mr. Sapiens Sapiens asking, 'Are you trying to teach me how to teach you?'

"I am just an inmate and I should hope whatever the staff members are doing is what they were taught to do. As you said we need to think in the context of a correction centre."

"Come on, why do I feel you are using my words to hedge my questions? Look, I truly endeavour to make a difference. It is a tough call, only possible when I have the true picture."

"Madam, perhaps my answers don't appeal to you but they are honest answers."

She looked at me for a long moment. "I think we are through. Thanks," she said eventually.

The visit was to haunt me a day later.

"We have an Iscariot," Matendechero said.

There was a chorus. "What?"

Matendechero was a bright fellow who studied early and late and always came tops. He was incurably selfish and had some books that he read when everyone else was away. He stood up and started pacing.

"There is a traitor." He kept his voice monotonously low. "Ask yourself; the manager beat us to the director's office. How did she know? The traitor sold us out. He also sold out Mwenda and Odeny."

"Who is the rascal?" Mpe, a huge bully from the Coast wanted to know.

"Who is he?"

"We want to lynch him!"

Matendechero stopped theatrically, then continued to pace studying the faces. He stopped near me and our eyes locked for a long moment. "What were you doing in the manager's office yesterday?"

Four very angry boys surrounded me. I was so mad I could hardly speak. "Exactly what do you want?"

"The truth," Matendechero said.

"Yes! That is what we want to know!" Mpe barked.

"She also invited me into the office," someone said and we all turned. It was Junge. "She wanted to know how she can serve us better."

The classroom fell silent like a tomb. I looked at Matendechero, who appeared confused.

"Why you two?" he asked.

"Why don't we ask the manager?" Junge said.

"How do we know whether that is actually what you talked about?" Mpe wanted to know.

"That is simple. Ask her," Junge said, getting on his feet. He started towards Matendechero. "What makes you behave as if you are the only one who is aggrieved? I clearly don't see how you stand to gain from witch-hunting. We clearly face more worthy enemies than one another; no books, no teachers and a society out there which is ready to lynch us at the slightest provocation. We only have one weapon: the fire to succeed. That is why we risked going to the director's office. That is why Mwenda and Odeny are not with us today. That is why, when we were offered freedom, we didn't jump at it. Indeed, we were afraid of it. We have a God-given chance to cement

133

our future. I cannot say that we are compatible; indeed it is irrational to expect such. But we have come this far. It is only a short while, then we go our different ways. As of now, we need one another's company more than one another's room. When I answer your question, I learn from it. When you improve and beat me, I am challenged to work harder and, as a result, we all become better. A candle loses nothing by lighting another candle, neither do you run faster by crippling your opponent."

Junge's long speech achieved the intended purpose because tempers went down and we resumed our studies.

Later on, I tracked Junge down and found him sunbathing.

"You lied," I said.

"I had to," he said. "They were baying for your blood.'

"So you gave them the task of beating the two of us. They dared not because you are a martial arts expert. That was ingenious. I was lucky I had confided in you."

"Matendechero is intelligent but incurably selfish. You stepped on his toes by almost becoming number one last term and he is not happy about it. He is determined to remain the star by hook or crook. The rest of us should only sing in his praise. I am not the cleverest in this class, but I know bedevilling anyone cannot improve my IQ."

"You are a true friend."

"Don't bank on it. Next time, I might not be in a position to save you. Just watch your step."

"Then you gave a profound speech.'

"You see, you are young and wild. I am not. Don't ask me about my age because I don't know it. All I know is that I am not your age. While young, I did bad things and got away with it too often. To my peers, I was a hero; the most notorious, the untouchable. Well, my fortieth day came and here I am. The truth is, if anyone knew my true age I could have joined a borstal or a real prison. This place has given me an opportunity to meditate and make hard decisions. Now I see things in a different light. There is a pattern emerging. I have a chance to make things right. I am not proud of my father. He certainly was too hard on me and I became deviant. Eager to prove him wrong, I ran away from home and became a criminal. I don't want my son to end up like me. I want him to be proud of his father."

"You have a son?"

"And a wife."

I looked at him with renewed interest. To my young mind, it appeared he had achieved so much.

"How is your father?" he asked.

"I never had one."

"Oh," he muttered. "That is tough."

We were silent for a long moment. "So how do we get the best out of this place?" Junge asked. That too was a hard question. By the time we joined form four, we had not covered a lot of the form three syllabus and superhuman effort was needed to make up for lost time and cover form four work before exams. We had no teacher for commerce. There was no indication that the future would be brighter than the past. Indeed it looked gloomy.

"We should work hard," I said. "Very hard."

I decided to revise widely. I would allocate myself tests from revision books and if I could not answer a particular question, I would visit the main text for proper reading. We were allowed to stay in class for preps until eight in the night. I would carry notes to the hostel and push myself up to nine when the lights were put out. There was so much to cover, it seemed unmanageable. Learning materials remained scarce and we continued losing teaching staff. Despite her consultations, the manager did nothing notable to salvage the situation.

Junge was always beside me. His attitude and determination was phenomenal, but then he was not academically gifted. I encouraged him to ask questions but he considered it a bother. He would ask me a question and after getting an answer, he would hastily say that he had understood.

"Is that right?"

"Why doubt me? I will perform so well they will feature me in the papers," he would say.

"That will be a big day for your son."

"Yeah," he would say thoughtfully. "I will be the proudest father in the world."

However, I would ask a similar question and he would fail to answer.

"A candle loses nothing by lighting another candle, remember?" I would tell him.

"How can I forget?"

Unlike the Othaya class, there was lack of togetherness. The expulsion of Mwenda and Odeny had dealt a major blow to the team spirit. Again, the class population was bigger with diverse personalities. Selfishness could not be overlooked as inmates sought individual glory. In the front line was Matendechero who wanted to pass and see others fail in equal measure. Basically, it was everyone for himself.

I cannot say I was fully prepared by the time the exams began; time just ran out. To my surprise, the exam covered most of the areas I had drilled myself on. Maybe luck was on my side or probably I had not appreciated how much energy I had put in the preparations. As the exams went on, I gained more confidence and by the time I floored the last paper, I felt I had given it my best shot.

Finishing the exam meant that finally, after nine long years, I was a free man. I recalled how I had yearned for this moment. I had always imagined it would be blissful. However, now that it had come, I only felt relieved. I reached for the release form in my pocket. Somehow it didn't feel right that I should prove to every misguided police officer that I had duly earned my freedom. As they say, some prisons don't have walls.

Across the road was Getathuru, rusty with age and neglect. A matatu stopped and a policeman alighted in the company of a young boy. Well, another boy's journey had just begun.

Armed with my books, five hundred and thirty seven shillings which I had earned in nine years, I flagged down a matatu to town. The ride to town brought back memories of my journey to the reception centre nine years before. Back then, everything had seemed strange but now it was familiar - from the boom boom of matatus to *chokoras*. Despite eloquent talks to rid the town of the oil-stained boys, they continued to rule the streets. They were a manifestation of a failed society: lost family values, unwanted pregnancies, abandoned parental responsibilities – a tragic mirror image of what I would have become had that Land Rover not appeared on that fateful day. High on sniffing glue, petrol and ignorance, some rested on heaps of trash like tourists on the beach.

As usual, human traffic hurried on, ignoring the gang they had created against themselves, which grew stronger by the day. They were once called 'street children'; now they were 'street families', next they would be 'street clans'. I concurred fully with the Children Services Director's observation that thousands of young boys could have been in our place in the programme. Where were the men in the government Land Rover? Why were they not arresting the oil-stained urchins? I wondered.

A *chokora* in a long overcoat was walking ahead of me down River Road, his attention riveted on the handbag of a lady a few paces ahead of him. I turned back, instinctively, apprehensive that another one was aiming at the polythene bag I was carrying. I tightened my grip on it, and then turned to the lady ahead intending to warn her. Before I could say, 'amen' the vagabond snatched the handbag and broke into a run.

"Help! Thief! Thief!" The lady's shrill voice cut the air. Events started unfolding like lightning. Idlers suddenly became active as if released from a binding spell; those who were busy found their tasks less urgent and abandoned them. They were all blood-thirsty. A sickening premonition seized me. The vagabond was clearly outnumbered and only a miracle was going to save him.

"Kill him!'

"Lynch the rascal!"

A miracle did not happen and the thief was caught. It was instant justice in one of its roughest jackets. In a record five minutes, he was arrested, sentenced and mercilessly beaten. Some people immediately left for their tasks while idlers hung by waiting for the next victim.

As I walked past the thief, I was able to have a closer look at him. My heart almost stopped as I recognised him. It was Karanchu! His legs and arms were broken, his skull had gaping wounds. He lay in a pool of blood. He was in a lot of pain. His eyes opened slightly and our eyes locked. He must have recognised me because he struggled to move his lips. However, whatever he wanted to say died with him as his limbs kicked violently then went still.

I had not witnessed anyone die before and it was horrible for someone I knew so well to be the first. The scene depressed my soul. It meant that the seven years Karanchu had spent in the correction institution was a waste of time and resources. Who was to blame, the management, his genes, or were some people born to live a turbulent life then die young? How many had ended up like Karanchu upon earning back their freedom?

I turned and started for Machakos Bus Station.

# CHAPTER 21

"Njoki!" Kazi Bure called immediately I alighted from the route 118 bus. Something crossed my mind and I smiled. KB had called me by my mother's name and I didn't mind at all. Back at Kiambiriria I would have made a face, called him names or even exchanged blows.

"You are the hero," KB went on excitedly. "I hear you passed."

"Is that it?" I asked, my heart racing. KB could not be expected to possess finer details as far as education excellence was concerned. Despite having been to school, KB was illiterate. To him, one just failed or passed, hence I headed to the office to know just how well I had passed.

To get to the secondary section offices, I had to pass by the manager's office. "Ssshhh!" I heard a voice and turned to see her calling me from the window of her office. I turned and headed to her office. After greetings she offered me a chair.

"Congratulations! You did us proud. It is fantastic to be sending a student to the university."

"You are welcome."

Apparently, I had passed so well I would be joining the university. The possibility was beyond my wildest dreams. I had certainly focused so much on my weakness that I wasn't able to appreciate my strength. To substantiate her words, the manager handed me a copy of the results. It was all there in black and white: I had scored a B plain! Matendechero came second with C plain. Junge had managed a C-. Well, he had not been featured in the papers but I was proud of him. I hoped his son was.

As other members of staff came to the office, each had something to say.

"I knew you would pass," one said.

"You should give tips to the current class on how to go about it," another one said.

"I know it's a challenge joining the university," the manager said. "I hope the Higher Education Loans Board will consider you."

I was leaving the manager's office when I saw Matendechero walking from the secondary section. He looked downcast. I joined him and we walked towards the gate.

"You did well," he said.

"You too," I cursed under my breath because my words sounded hollow.

"You say that to comfort me."

His sincerity was touching, but then it could not change a thing. It only reminded me of pointless battles, wasted

142

energies and lost opportunities. It reminded me of our failure to pull together towards a common goal.

"We did what we had to do."

"I wish we could do it all over again," he said. His voice was full of emotion. "I could have done better, my approach was poor."

We both knew that this was true. He was not a C grade student. My performance was better but shouting it out was improper. The issue of winning or losing was immaterial because, to me, the main objective was to equip oneself with the ability to face the future with confidence.

"So now you will join the university."

"Perhaps. I don't have funds and I don't see them starting an approved university soon."

"I wish you all the best," he said stretching his hand. I took it and shook it. "You too."

I stood outside the gate imagining myself in the university. I felt I should feel the real thing and walked to Lower Kabete campus of the University of Nairobi. No one was in uniform and I quickly blended with the students. The first thing that hit me was the easy air about the place. No one was in a hurry, no bell sounded. I discovered they were all communicating in English, something that made me apprehensive. I had passed my exam but still I could not communicate fluently in the language.

Then I came upon a strange couple. The girl donned the shortest miniskirt I had ever seen. She was naked from armpits upward, her brief top being held in place by her heavy breasts. The man had one leg of his jeans pants cut-off at the knee. The bold writing on his T-shirt read: MAD NOT STUPID. He wore a pair of earrings and his hair was beautifully plaited. The man had one arm on the girl's shoulder. I was taken aback. Were they really students? I wondered. After loitering for half an hour, I left.

I arrived home to a changed society. Everyone wanted to know if indeed it was true I had done well and how I had managed it. Evidently, the results were contrary to their expectations.

"You will now join the university!" someone said.

"Do you mean you didn't pay a single cent?"

"How can I enrol my son in the institution?"

"Do they enrol girls?"

Others communicated with their eyes. However, this time round it was different. They did not accuse or rebuke, they appreciated me. Even Anastasia was not left out.

"How is the going?" she asked.

"Smooth, I would say." She looked at me long and hard.

"It appears I was wrong about your school."

"Why?"

"Your performance."

I had nothing to say about that.

"You have been avoiding me since that day," she observed.

"Maybe I have nothing to tell you."

"Really?"

"I don't think we should talk about it," I said and I detected an edge on my voice. "Besides, you are occupied."

She raised her eyebrows. "Occupied?"

"Jeff."

A weak smile appeared on her lips. "We were not lovers. It was our first date and I wanted to see if we could match." She was thoughtful for a long moment. "But then you are right. Let's forget it."

She was moody but no longer contemptuous. She had a *leso* thrown over her shoulders. I could tell something was troubling her but I didn't care to know what it was. I had long decided that we were not compatible and I had no desire to force it. I did not love or hate her; she was just another girl. The feelings that had once threatened to consume me had long subsided. I was stronger, I was my own master.

Something was bothering me, though. The people we met on the way looked at me as if I had a wooden nose. I had grown used to many things, but I would never get used to the way people communicated with their eyes. The danger was in misinterpreting the message. Anastasia's company made me feel uncomfortable and I took a different path.

I recalled my first day in school and, as usual, I smiled. I recalled how my mother was infuriated when I failed the interview and how I had not understood the cause of her rage. Now I understood perfectly. I held my left ear with my right hand over my head and my smile broadened. Well, one day I will carry out a research to establish the relationship between the length of an arm, the size of a head and education, I thought. It was a pity that my mother, the person who would have been the happiest, was no more. She would not have asked if it was true or how I had managed it because she had believed in me. I looked at the skies above. She was up there celebrating.

My mind travelled to the three men who had forcibly taken me from my mother's house and to their boss at the children's office. The old man's voice rang in my mind. "One day you will understand." Where were they? I wanted to tell them I understood and urge them to be gentler to the next victim. I was happy because my mother had understood before she died. That is why she had urged me to stay put.

I felt greatly indebted to Agnes. I didn't know how to thank her because she had helped me so much. Sometimes I wondered whether she was attracted to me. I fought to convince myself that her actions were purely aimed at assisting me in my studies. This was not an easy task keeping in mind that I was a lonely man and she was a beautiful girl. I had hoped to meet her when I was returning her books. On arrival at her home I found her mother splitting firewood. She stopped and studied me carefully.

"I am returning these books to Agnes." She took the books, looking at me suspiciously.

"Is she home?"

"No."

"Tell her I am very grateful. Hey, can I assist you with that?" I had said, pointing at the log.

"Sure," she said loosening up. Within twenty minutes, I was on my way home.

# CHAPTER 22

All was well until it was Patrick's turn to congratulate me. My cousin could be comical when he wanted to and he promptly assumed the role of a television presenter. He clenched his fist and turned it into a microphone.

"Congratulations!" he exclaimed. "The viewers can hardly wait to hear from you. To what can you attribute your success?" he brought the fist to my face.

"Determination, resilience and ..."

"Thank you," he cut me short. "What will you call the newborn?" he asked and I gave him a vacant look. "It is an open secret already, you know."

"What secret?" I yelled.

"Anastasia, of course!"

Then it hit me. Anastasia was expecting! That explained her mood, the *leso* and the changed attitude. I wiped Patrick's fist from my face. "This is not funny."

"Are you telling me…?" he started.

"I am telling you nothing!"

"Calm down, okay?"

I was so mad I thought of paying Anastasia a visit and telling her off. Were Patrick and company only inferring or was she telling them that I was responsible?

Apparently, her attitude towards me had changed when she fell pregnant and she had hoped I would be foolish enough to approach her and ensnare myself. But I did not. She had become desperate and started accusing me of avoiding her.

Then, as if on cue, Anastasia appeared from nowhere hurrying towards us, carrying a travelling bag. She looked rattled and it was clear she had been crying. The lustre of her beauty was no longer breathtaking. Indeed, she looked older. She came to an abrupt stop, her eyes oscillating between the two of us.

"I have come to stay," she declared in a feeble voice.

"Why did…?" I started.

"I told you…," Patrick ventured.

"Save your breath," she hissed venomously and walked past us and into Patrick's cabin. I turned sharply to Patrick who looked as though he had survived a heart attack.

"I don't understand," I confessed.

"I am sorry," he said and his face dropped. "I thought you were in the race too. It seemed like every man was after her. A dozen men could be the father of that child. Why on earth should I be victimised? It was only once, for heaven's sake!"

"You wanted to marry her, right?"

"No."

"No?" I asked. "Then what were you doing messing up with her?"

He stared at me long and hard. "Do you suffer from erectile dysfunction? Good grief, that is gross. I am sorry."

"What happened to Nelly?"

"Nothing," he had a faraway look. "Trouble is when they are all born beautiful."

"That is not true," I said. "Trouble is when you want them all."

He sat on a nearby stone. He was on the verge of tears. "How did it come to this? Look at me, I have nothing. I have to depend on my parents to eat. But I lie to every beautiful girl and promise them the world. Heaven knows why they buy my lies. It is a crazy world where lies are misconstrued as truth. Trouble is, my life itself has become a lie. I admire you, honestly. You see, you can face the world with confidence. I have been reckless. Not only with her but many others. Just the other day, they were showing a film at the village about AIDS. Do you know what? I could not watch because I felt as though they were talking about my life."

He broke down without warning. "I am not ready to die," he sobbed.

I must confess that I am not good at soothing. I watched him disintegrate, hopelessly raking through my mind for something apt to say or do. I wished I had some training in counselling. He was no longer the carefree Patrick I knew. He was finally willing to face his sense of worthlessness. The last time I saw him shed a tear was twelve years before. The breakdown was a culmination of a devastating turmoil which must have been killing him by and by. I placed my hands on his shoulders and squatted in front of him. "Look, you only think that you are infected. No one said that you have AIDS or any other disease for that matter. There is only one way to find out."

"VCT," he muttered and I nodded. His eyes dropped and he ran his hand through his hair. "It is scary, isn't it?"

"I will be the first."

He lifted his eyes, searched my face and I nodded encouragingly. Without uttering a word, he collected himself then started towards the gate and I followed him. His tone, his swagger and general carriage suggested a beaten man. His parents were not at home and I dreaded their come-back. I didn't know whether my suggestion to visit a VCT centre would tone things down or aggravate the situation. My decision had been abrupt and I considered its ramifications as we walked. I had not been reckless like my cousin, but there were always other ways of contracting a dangerous disease. But then there was only one way to find out.

I admired Patrick's confidence. For once, he seemed really engrossed. He was generally a shallow person, an attribute that was repulsive at times. But he could be resolute. I couldn't tell what was going on in his mind, but judging from his determination, he was not concerned about the outcome of the test. He seemed to have acquired some new power that kept him a step ahead of me.

"Where is Jeff?" I ventured in an attempt to keep my mind off what was about to take place.

"His father was transferred."

We didn't have to go all the way to town. The Administration Police unit had pitched tent on the outskirts of the town. A lady AP welcomed and introduced us to three other boys in the tent. Another officer took over and declared we would have a brief discussion.

"Thank you for paying us a visit. Feel most welcome," she said, addressing the two of us. "You have made a bright decision this day to know your HIV status. It is the first step to a better tomorrow for you and the society in general."

My mind was preoccupied, but I was able to grasp the thread of her discourse.

"Contrary to the common fear, being HIV positive is not a death warrant. It is only an indication that you need to take care of your health in a more informed manner. If you are negative, then you need to embrace ABC. Abstain if you are not married; be faithful to one partner if you are married. If these two fail, use a condom. We are obligated to fight this pandemic, and the most important weapon is the very way we live. Let's learn to live."

Patrick's eyes were closed, most certainly trying to fight emotions in his heart. The man in front of me glided the soles of his shoes on the floor every now and then. He would then cup his face in his hands as if in a silent prayer.

The lady concluded her discussion.

"Forcing one to take the test so that they can be employed is illegal, isn't it?" the man in front of me asked in a thick, shaky voice. He was definitely posing the question to the wrong person because I was not an authority in legal matters. In answer, I simply shrugged my shoulders.

I found myself thinking failure was a good thing. I thought of all those girls whom I had admired and something told me maybe I was alive because I had failed to win them. However, the feeling went too far because I found myself wishing the testing machines would fail....

The man in front of me sighed audibly, glided his soles noisily and collected himself to his feet. He didn't walk out of the tent; he ran. That meant I was next. I looked at the vacant seat and couldn't muster the courage to occupy it. The curtain to where blood samples were being collected moved and an AP officer beckoned me inside. The doctor's little talk did very little to sooth my nerves as he collected my blood sample. I was sweating like a leaking roof.

# CHAPTER 23

It was almost three. Despite my protestations, Patrick stormed Watering Point Pub. He was spellbound by emotions so much he could hardly talk. Now and then, he wiped a tear off his face. He ordered a beer and I ordered a cold Coke.

"Wow!" he shouted. "I am HIV negative!"

The waitress smiled and her eyes travelled to a sticker on the wall that read: Even if you have been tested I am not interested.

"That is fine with me!" Patrick retorted. Tears were now streaming down his face. I couldn't blame him. Personally, I felt as though I had woken from a very bad nightmare. I just could not believe I had mustered the confidence to go through the test. I was not crying like my cousin, but I felt relieved beyond words.

"You know, taking that test was a bright idea," Patrick said. "Scary but bright."

Something occurred to me as I watched him sip his beer. It was ridiculous but I had to know.

"Do you smoke marijuana?" I ventured.

"No. Why?"

"To assist you face the girls."

Patrick looked stupefied. "Why on earth should I? I lie, period. Lies, lies and more lies."

There was no point narrating about Karanchu. The two had used their charm with the girls but poor Karanchu had used marijuana to fight stigma.

"You are newly married, remember? Married men get home early," I said.

"Home is the last place I want to be."

We were walking back home when a car stopped a few meters ahead of us. The driver leaned out of the window facing us. At first I did not recognise him.

"Jeff!" Patrick exclaimed. His shock was physical. "What in heaven's name are you doing here?"

"Get in," he said, opening the door for us. He had changed so much. Probably he was swollen all over because he could not have gained so much weight so fast. He was in a cream suit, a black shirt and black suede shoes. A pair of sunglasses rested on his clean-shaven scalp.

"Sorry, I am a bit tied up...," Patrick stammered looking at me for support. I couldn't think of something proper to say in time. He entered the car clumsily and I followed him.

"You are still stuck here, eh?" Jeff said as he pulled off. "You should come to Nairobi. That is where life is, you know. Countryside is a drag."

"I am considering it," Patrick said. "What do you do?"

"Business. We fell apart with my old man. He is a dinosaur, you know. He still believes children are born to get degrees. What a drag. I am not a bookworm, you know. It is my time to get rich or die trying."

"What brings you here?"

"Anastasia."

"Who?" Patrick asked. He had overreacted and Jeff turned to face him sharply. Personally, I was taken aback because Anastasia had confessed that she was not in an affair with Jeff. The sensitivity of the situation did not escape my attention. Here were two men sharing a girl and one of them, based purely on lies, had impregnated the girl.

"I thought you split," Patrick said.

"Split?"

"Things have been happening, you know," Patrick said.

Jeff was losing his patience now. He swerved the car to the road side and stopped the engine. "What things?" Patrick had lost his voice.

"What he means is that something happened to her," I said.

"Is she dead…?"

"No, no, no. Nothing so terrible," Patrick said.

"Then what?"

"She, ah, she was chased from her home by her parents," I said wondering why I was covering my cousin.

"Is that it?"

"Well, it is a little more complicated," I said.

"I am listening."

"Look. Why don't you just go and forget about her?" Patrick said.

"How dare you! She is the love of my life," his eyes narrowed to slits. "Have you been…?"

"No. I mean…"

"Has this to do with the pregnancy?"

Patrick's mouth hung open.

"Ah, eh, yes," I said.

"It is my mistake," Jeff said. "Initially, I thought marrying her was a crazy idea and I denied responsibility."

Patrick ventured to say something and I almost told him to shut up.

"This is an honourable thing, I mean, taking care of your child," I said.

Twenty minutes later, we were entering Patrick's cabin. Anastasia was asleep in his bed and he woke her up.

"Hello darling," Jeff said. "I have come for you." Anastasia had lost interest in the two of us and she collected her items ready to leave.

"You are a true friend. Thank you for the refuge," she told Patrick while accompanying Jeff to the car. Her statement was a shrewd way of creating the impression that Patrick had only given her a place to stay. Patrick was irate but he managed to contain himself.

"I know that look," I said. "You are mad because she has proved to be a better liar."

"You bet I am! Whatever the case, it is good riddance," he said entering his cabin as I followed him. "What a day! I woke up convinced that I was dying, then I was given my life back. I got married by force and four hours later, I was divorced," he laughed. "Good grief!"

Just then, Nelly appeared at the door. Apparently she had heard the news, judging from the shocked look. She was in a pair of faded jeans trousers, a hooded sweatshirt and a pair of sandals. I had last met her during the outing to Karia dam. Then, she had been buoyant but today she looked downcast. She didn't greet us but stood there looking at us with hatred. Patrick's guilt paralysed him. Tears started oozing from her eyes. A tear dropped then sobs shook her body.

"I am sorry…," Patrick started but she turned and started off effectively cutting him short. He dashed after her. I had had enough drama for one day and I decided to have a stroll away from it all. I stopped outside the gate contemplating which way to go. To the right Patrick and Nelly were fighting it out and this forced me to take a left turn. Before I could turn, Agnes came from round the bend. I was somehow pleasantly surprised to see her. She walked past the two arguing lovers and stopped near me.

"Are they patching up or breaking up?" she asked.

"It is hard to tell," I retorted. We started walking.

"Ever had a girlfriend?" she asked.

"No," She turned to look at me searchingly. "Ever had a boyfriend?"

She was silent for a long moment. "Yes. However, all I have to show for it is a broken heart. It looks like the true meaning of love was lost long before we were born."

Her answer had dampened her spirits and she looked downcast. "What does love mean to you?"

The question had me thinking.

"I think it is a strong desire between two persons for mutual wellbeing, driven by a deep understanding of the other person and built on an unqualified acceptance of their strengths and – more importantly – weaknesses. Friction is bound to occur. Of concern is whether it breaks or builds you."

She made a face jokingly. "Am I repeating the questions in KCSE? By the way, congratulations."

"Which reminds me. I was so unkind to you. I am so sorry."

"It was nothing," she said.

"The books helped a lot. Thanks."

"Welcome."

We walked in silence. My mind had suddenly gone blank. However, I was satisfied just walking next to her. A car was approaching and I identified it as that of her father. It pulled up near us.

"I heard you did remarkably well," her father said.
"Congratulations."

"Thank you, sir."

He then turned to his daughter. I expected him to say something but he just accelerated and sped off.

"This sun will bake us alive. What do you think?" Agnes said.

"We have survived it before. We only forget too fast."

"Do you always give the same answers?"

"Do you always ask the same questions?"

Our eyes locked and she laughed.

# CHAPTER 24

I was going through my documents when I saw my release form. To complete the release process, I was to present the form to the District Children's Services Office. I decided to visit the office on a Monday. My journey to the office brought back memories of how it all began. My excitement grew with every step I took. Why, I was about to meet the men who arrested me! I could not remember what the three men in the Land Rover looked like, but their boss, the man with the receding hairline and traces of grey hair, was somehow imbedded in my mind. I was also excited at the prospect of knowing the identity of the person who had engineered my arrest. Facts pointed an accusing finger at Patrick's father, but I needed to confirm it from the horse's mouth.

The Land Rover that transported me to this place eight years ago was parked next to two other broken down vehicles outside the office. Rotten leaves and flowers from the huge jacaranda tree that spread above them formed a fertile layer from where weeds thrived. In the office, a young lady was busy hammering away at a typewriter, simultaneously whistling the song *Malaika* by Fadhili Williams. She greeted me, her fingers still flying on the keyboard.

"I am here to see the District Children's Services Officer," I said loudly to counter the clatter from her machine.

"What for?"

I gave her the release form. "Walk right in."

My heart sank the moment I entered the small office. The man seated across the table looking at me expectantly was young and a total stranger. It meant that I would never know the person who was responsible for my arrest.

"How can I help you?" the man asked. "Have a seat."

I gave him the release form. He pulled a drawer and removed a rubber stamp. He stamped the form, signed it and threw the carbon copy into the out tray.

"You are a changed person now, I believe?" he said handing back my copy.

I nodded.

"Be good," he said opening a file. I had so many questions to ask but didn't know how and where to start. The man looked at me questioningly. "Is there anything else?"

"Yes. I …." I trailed off as a bespectacled man in a black pinstriped suit walked into the office. I recognised him at once. His hair was all grey now but I had no difficulty in recognising him.

"Do you remember me, sir?" I asked greeting the man. He appeared lost and I handed him the release form. He glanced at the form as his face beamed.

"Muthini Njoki!" he exclaimed removing his spectacles. "Of course I remember you!"

He grabbed my hand and shook it energetically. "How can I forget you? Our first meeting was not very cordial," the man said. "I am Mr. Wanderi, the serving District Children's Services Officer. You are grown up now. So, how was it?"

"I sat for KCSE and scored B plain."

The man across the table looked at me with new respect.

"That is great!" Mr. Wanderi exploded. "I knew I was right about you. Are you through with Mr. Wanjohi?" he said referring to the young man. I nodded. "Wait for me at my car. I won't be long."

Mr. Wanderi joined me ten minutes later and we drove to town. "I am retired now. I am so happy when I meet young men like you who benefited from my services."

"Why did you come for me?"

"Your mother."

"What?" I said in disbelief. How could he say that? It was preposterous! My mother had fought the men who arrested me. If only she had the ability, I would not have been taken away. It was impossible to think of her as the perpetrator of my arrest.

"Your mother visited my office several times with your report forms and demand letters from your former school. She wanted the office to settle your fees arrears. Many parents visited us with same demands but the office has no mandate to pay school fees. Two years later, one of my retired colleagues who hailed from your home area reported that you had dropped out of school for almost two years. He also explained at length the situation at your home."

"My mother did not want me to go," I protested. "In fact, your men took me away by force."

"That is true," Mr. Wanderi said, changing gear. "To her, indeed to many people, approved schools were for criminals. As the situation stood, I had to take action with or without her consent. I decided to put you under care and protection."

My mother's sentiment during our last moments together in Kericho augmented Mr. Wanderi's account. She had said, "This is not how I would have wanted it, but it seems the only way."

"She visited some years ago and reported that you were doing well in Kericho. She was so happy. How is she?"

The question brought back memories of my uncle and grandmother's visit at Othaya with the news of my mother's demise.

"She passed on."

"I am so sorry. She was a wonderful woman."

We stopped outside Silvergate Hotel, the best hotel in town. As if in consensus to observe a minute of silence in honour of my mother's departed soul, silence fell between us for several moments.

"Come on," Mr. Wanderi said. "This is a big day. Let's go and celebrate!"

We entered the big hotel.

The End